Everyone Hates Kelsie Miller

Also by Meredith Ireland

The Jasmine Project

Everyone Hates Kelsie Miller

Meredith Ireland

SIMON & SCHUSTER BFYR

NEW YORK LONDON TORONTO SYDNEY NEW DELHI

For Laura and for anyone

who has lost a best friend

SIMON & SCHUSTER BFYR

An imprint of Simon & Schuster Children's Publishing Division
1230 Avenue of the Americas, New York, New York 10020
This book is a work of fiction. Any references to historical events, real people, or real places are used fictitiously.
Other names, characters, places, and events are products of the author's imagination, and any resemblance
to actual events or places or persons, living or dead, is entirely coincidental.
Text © 2022 by Meredith Ireland
Jacket illustration and design © 2022 by Sandra Chiu
Interior map © 2022 by Bethany Lord
All rights reserved, including the right of reproduction in whole or in part in any form.
SIMON & SCHUSTER BOOKS FOR YOUNG READERS
and related marks are trademarks of Simon & Schuster, Inc.
For information about special discounts for bulk purchases, please contact Simon & Schuster
Special Sales at 1-866-506-1949 or business@simonandschuster.com.
The Simon & Schuster Speakers Bureau can bring authors to your live event.
For more information or to book an event, contact the Simon & Schuster Speakers Bureau
at 1-866-248-3049 or visit our website at www.simonspeakers.com.
Interior design by Tom Daly
The text for this book was set in Adobe Caslon Pro.
Manufactured in the United States of America
First Edition
2 4 6 8 10 9 7 5 3 1
Library of Congress Cataloging-in-Publication Data
Names: Ireland, Meredith, author.
Title: Everyone hates Kelsie Miller / Meredith Ireland.
Description: First edition. | New York : Simon & Schuster Books for Young Readers, [2022] |
Audience: Ages 12+. | Audience: Grades 7–9. | Summary: Kelsie and Eric, rivals for valedictorian, team
up to go on an overnight road trip to the University of Pennsylvania to win back their exes.
Identifiers: LCCN 2021050960 (print) | LCCN 2021050961 (ebook) |
ISBN 9781665906975 (hardcover) | ISBN 9781665906999 (ebook)
Subjects: CYAC: Dating (Social customs)—Fiction. | Best friends—Fiction. | Friendship—Fiction. |
High schools—Fiction. | Schools—Fiction. | Korean Americans—Fiction. | LCGFT: Novels.
Classification: LCC PZ7.1.I743 Ev 2022 (print) | LCC PZ7.1.I743 (ebook) | DDC [Fic]—dc23
LC record available at https://lccn.loc.gov/2021050960
LC ebook record available at https://lccn.loc.gov/2021050961

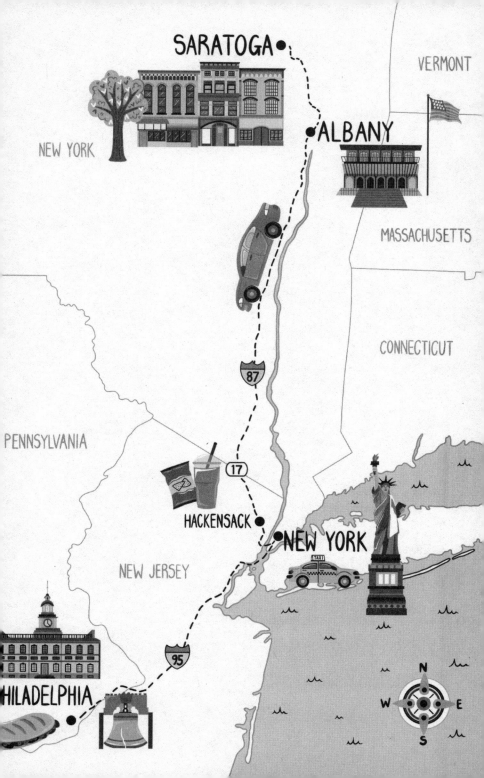

CHAPTER ONE

My parents love this old song where the girl knows down to the hour how long her lover has been gone. I'd never come close to feeling that way about some dude, but I had the same tragic energy as I missed my best friend.

It'd been twenty-two hours and thirty-six days since I'd last seen Brianna. Two hours and thirty days since she'd last responded to my texts—not that I was painfully aware of the time to the minute or anything.

But second after lonely second had passed, and somehow it was another Saturday night in our small town—or, I should say, my small town. Brianna Hoffman had moved across the country to Seattle, so it wasn't like Saratoga was "ours" any-more. Yet it was still a summer weekend, and I had plans.

I was acting like a saddo at a house party.

All around me girls shouted elaborate toasts before spill-ing shots down their gullets. Future frat boys showed off their flip-cup skills in the dining room, hoping for the girls to notice them. Guys who were way too old for high school parties creeped in the corner of the living room. And in the kitchen, a crowd was celebrating someone eating a full can of whipped cream in record time.

It was the worst place on earth to be sad.

But I'd gone in with a mission.

It just wasn't working out.

I stood alone by the sliding-glass door, nursing the contents of my red Solo cup while repeatedly scanning the party. The mystery green punch tasted like apples and aftershave, but the liquor had made taking a duck-faced selfie marginally bearable. I'd posted it online in a pathetic attempt to say: Look how I'm having fun without you! Like Brianna was even going to check my socials.

"Oh em gee, we should do karaoke!" some girl screeched. Like that. Like the letters—O. M. and, you guessed it, G.

"Hell yeah!" was the reply.

No.

I tossed my cup and slid out into the backyard. I could handle only so much in my fragile state. It was dark, but it wouldn't be too dark to wander the few blocks home. Crushing loneliness aside, it was a perfect night. The humidity had dropped, and the late August air held the crispness of the impending fall.

I paused on the deck and let out a long exhale, both glad to be free and bummed my plan had been a resounding failure.

I'd even tried to look cute—like my headband/sundress combo was going to clinch it with Teagan, my other former friend. We'd been friends through Bri, and I'd also lost her when Bri left. But I figured Teagan would be so wowed by my fashion sense that we'd be friends again and she'd immediately tell me why she and Brianna had ghosted me.

It was foolproof.

All right, it was more wishful thinking than a plan, but I was running low on options. I'd tried messaging, calling, a hyper-aggressive unsolicited FaceTime, Snaps, and commenting on every one of Bri's Instagram posts, and none of it had worked.

I started to move again and was almost to the edge of the deck when I felt the vibration of my phone. I rummaged around my purse, missing my cell over and over again in the small bag.

Was it Bri? Please be Bri.

My hands shook as I tried to unlock the screen, over-eagerness getting the best of me. I cursed my lack of text previews and was on my second attempt to unlock my phone when my foot missed the top deck stair.

The thing about top steps is, they're crucial. Miss that one and the others don't matter much. So I went tumbling on down, only instead of hitting the ground, my fate was worse: I slammed into the broad chest of Eric Mulvaney Ortiz. And then we fell into a rosebush.

Yeah.

All six-foot-two of the star quarterback of our mediocre

football team and all five-foot-one of my should-be-valedic-torian-so-at-least-I-have-that got tangled up in an enormous rosebush.

"What the—" he said.

"Where did—" I said.

We paused a breath away from each other, noses almost touching. Eric smelled like charred wood and cologne with a touch of smugness. I smelled like lilacs and, I don't know, probably pariah.

I locked eyes with him, adrenaline coursing through my body. His heart was also beating fast, thumping through his T-shirt.

After an uncomfortable amount of time, he looked away and cleared his throat. "Oh, it's you," he said.

It was the kind of greeting you'd give a ladybug you don't want in your house but you won't kill because it'd be bad luck. I should mention here that we'd been rivals since kindergarten and not to throw around the word "nemesis" but . . . accurate.

We both tried to get up, but between my limbs, his, and the branches, we were hopelessly enmeshed. Eric fans from our high school would've killed to have been in my shoes, with him on top of me. I, however, just wanted out.

"Let me—" he said.

"If you would just—" I huffed.

Again I moved, but he shifted at the same time. He pulled my long hair, and I elbowed him in the ribs ("accidentally"), and we both stopped. Everything hurt and was only getting worse between the thorns and his heavy-ass limbs.

Eric was perennially in my way. As rising seniors, he was the one thing standing between me and a clear path to vale-dictorian. Of course he couldn't have been a brainless piece of muscle. Nooo. One, my life wasn't that easy, and two, our school didn't have any of those. Funded by eccentric billion-aire Jim Carver, Carver Preparatory High School, one of the best in the nation, was tuition-free but you needed a 93 aver-age in middle school just to be invited to apply. Eric and I had easily qualified with 100s from Saratoga Public Intermediate School. Then we'd ended junior year with 99.89s. Both of us.

I know. . . . Intolerable on many counts.

"Look, I'm going to stand and then I'll help you up," he said.

I didn't trust him. At all. But what choice did I have in the rosebush? The last thing I wanted was one of his football bros discovering us and snapping a pic. In a flash I saw the social media post of a Korean girl (me) making a doughnut-hole sur-prised mouth and his rumpled Irish-Dominican good looks with a #CaughtInTheAct type sticker.

No way. Death before dishonor.

I nodded and Eric managed to stand. As promised, he extended his arm and helped me to my feet. Once we were upright, we flung our hands apart and checked our phones.

Although I would've sworn on my little sister's life that I'd gotten a text, I had no new messages. From the look on Eric's face, whatever he'd expected wasn't there either. Probably his eight thousandth unneeded scholarship offer. Even though we were only juniors, the contest of who could get the most merit scholarships had already begun, as it did for upperclassmen every year.

Eric slid his phone into his pocket and smoothed himself out. We both had little scrapes on our arms and legs and bigger cuts on our hands. He sighed and pulled a tissue out of his pocket. Yes, Eric was a teenage boy who carried around a pack of Kleenex—like my grandma Mimi.

"Do you want one?" he asked.

I could've used one, but I shook my head no.

"Put some Neosporin on your hand when you get home," he said.

I doubted he actually cared about my risk of infection, but he wouldn't miss an opportunity to impart medical wisdom.

"Uh-huh," I said.

We idled in three seconds of awkward silence.

"What are you doing here, Miller?" he asked. Aside from Mr. Broadsword, our AP US History teacher, Eric was the only person who called me by my last name.

"Oh, you know, just waiting to sack the Hero of Carver," I said.

After the team barely won half their games last fall, the local newspaper still had the nerve to do a spotlight piece on Eric. They called him the "Hero of Carver"—hands down the most obnoxious thing I'd ever seen. And I had to see it every time I went in for a checkup since his doctor dad had laminated and framed it. In two spots in the waiting room.

Eric rolled his eyes at me. "I meant you're not usually at these types of things. Or dressed like that."

"Are you keeping track? I'm touched." I pointed to my chest and batted my eyes.

"Good talk," he said.

He turned but didn't step away, and for some reason I was relieved he lingered. Which was too weird because I hated him. HATED. But loneliness and the need to talk to someone . . . anyone who really knew me was rewiring my responses. Despite the soul-crushing unfairness of it all, Eric and I did know each other. Living in the same school district, we'd been in every class together since kindergarten and our parents were friends.

"I thought Teagan would be here," I muttered.

He raised his eyebrows and blinked a couple of times, like he couldn't imagine me speaking to him.

"She was earlier, but she bounced, like, half an hour ago," he said.

I gritted my teeth. So Teagan had come, and either she'd avoided me or me and my bad luck had missed her. Fabulous. Yet somehow I managed to have Eric all to myself, and that guy was never alone. Wait, why was he by himself?

"Were you hiding in the rosebush?" I asked.

"I wasn't hiding in the . . ." He sighed in a long, suffering way. "I was checking my phone and didn't see you."

"Nah, it's cool. If you want to lurk like a creeper in a kiddie park, who am I going to tell?" I said.

That drew another sigh. He ran his nonbleeding hand down his face. My mom liked to say he had "classic bone structure." I didn't understand what that meant, but he had a straight nose, a smooth forehead, and a square jaw. He hadn't even had an acne stage. Which . . . what kind of unfair bullshit was that? I used to have pimples on my nose with their own gravitational pull.

"I was looking for a message from my girlfriend," Eric finally said.

Ah, the girlfriend. The one who looked like a young Catherine Zeta-Jones. I knew all about her, even though she didn't go to Carver. Eric was the favorite subject of the school rumor mill, and he and some girl no one had met were suddenly dubbed *the* power couple over the summer. His girlfriend was a year older than us, an Instagram model with like a hundred thousand followers, and she was going into her freshman year at UPenn.

Note: I wasn't entirely convinced she was a real person. Even her name, "Jessica Lovelace," sounded fake, but whatever. If he wanted to have an imaginary girlfriend, that was his business.

"Oh," I said.

We locked into another conversational pause and both returned to our phones. To save you the suspense: I didn't have any new messages.

"How's Bri doing?" Eric asked.

Her name made my heart contract, and pain leaked through the hole in my chest created by her absence. I stared at him, trying to figure out if he was intentionally jabbing at me, but he seemed like he was genuinely asking.

"I don't know." The words tasted like sand in my mouth.

He looked puzzled for a second, squinting one of his hazel eyes. "She must be busy with settling in and all that. I can't imagine moving cross country and switching schools with one year left."

"Well, neither can I," I blurted out. "She hates me and won't talk to me."

Eric's eyes widened, and I regretted opening my mouth. I hadn't meant to kick off a little heart-to-heart with him, but I was exhausted. After a month of missing my other half, I wasn't at my best.

Then again, it wasn't like I was telling him anything top secret. School would pick up in a week and a half, and the rumor mill would eat up my excommunication from her and Teagan's friendship. I was surprised the news wasn't out already since there was no such thing as privacy at Carver, but maybe Eric had missed it since he'd been away at camp. Because he was eighteen and still went to sleepaway camp.

He shook his head like he hadn't heard me right. "Brianna Hoffman hates you?"

"Everyone hates me lately."

"Why?" he asked.

That was the million-dollar question. I didn't know. One night I'd gone to bed having a best friend, and the next day I didn't have one. I kept going over things in my head and couldn't figure out the answer. The last time I hung out with Bri was at her going-away party, and everything had been fine. For the most part. Plus, we'd texted for days after that, so it couldn't have been anything from the party. Yet once Bri landed in Seattle, it was like she and Teagan had been waiting to cut me off because I hadn't heard from either since. I needed to know what had happened, but neither of them would talk to me and that was as hurtful as it was frustrating.

"I really don't know," I said.

Eric stared at me for what felt like an eternity. With each creeping second, I felt more and more foolish. Why had I unburdened myself to him? He was the last person in the world who'd care. He'd snickered during my salutatorian speech in middle school. He'd spiked a volleyball at my head in freshman-year gym. He'd secretly requested extra-credit assignments to try to edge me out of the top GPA in sophomore year (before I learned to do that too). Yeah, we'd known each other since we were little kids, but he wasn't a friend or confidant. I was just desperate.

But not this frigging desperate.

I took a step to go around him. He put his muscular arm out, a yard from touching me, yet stopping me nonetheless. His fingers splayed, then he balled his hand in a fist and dropped it at his side. I looked up at him.

"Jessica hasn't messaged me since the day I came home from football camp," he said. "Almost three days now."

He spoke in a voice so low, I wasn't even sure I'd heard

him. But then it sank in. If my eyes could've bulged out of my head, they would've. Someone (other than me) didn't want Eric Mulvaney Ortiz? Seriously? His fan club was, like, 499 strong—and there were 500 students at Carver.

"She ghosted you?" I said.

The second the words were out of my mouth, I knew they were the wrong ones. Obviously he'd been ghosted, but it would've hurt to hear it.

He stood straighter and his expression changed.

"Never mind." He shoved both hands in his pockets.

Silence again.

Despite my general desire to stick it to Eric whenever I could, that was mostly at school and generally academic. I scrambled for words to smooth things over. I was overly familiar with how much it sucked to be ignored.

"I . . . I won't tell anyone," I said.

He shook his head. "Appreciate it. But it's not that I'm ashamed or anything. I'm worried about her."

I skewed my face. "Why?"

"UPenn is a lot, and she gets anxious. I think she pulled away because she's overwhelmed, but I can't help her because I can't reach her. I wish . . . I wish I could just see her to know she's okay, you know?"

I had no idea why he was telling me all that, but I did a hundred percent know that feeling.

"You and me both," I said. "I mean about Bri. I don't really care about your girlfriend—no offense."

"None taken."

I exhaled. "I check Bri's socials to see what she's doing and to know she's alive and I never used to have to do that. We'd pick out filters and backgrounds together before she even posted anything. It's awful being on the outside when I was in the inner circle my whole life."

"Since kindergarten," he said. Because of course he had to correct me.

I stomped my foot. "You know what I mean."

"I do," he said with a surprising amount of sincerity. "I look at Jessica's Insta all the time. I'm now overly familiar with the UPenn campus." He grimaced and stared at the patio paving stones.

"Well, according to her feed, Bri's visiting there next week," I said. "Hey, we should show up with roses for each of them." I reached out and touched the bush we'd seriously damaged.

I laughed, but he didn't. It wasn't surprising. Eric had the sense of humor of a moldy turnip. But his eyes took on a startling intensity. His lips parted, but I couldn't hear him because he was cut off by an owl hoot. Not a real owl. We're the Carver Owls (a wise bird and the worst mascot in history), and it was one of his teammates.

"Yo, Ortiz, where you at?" Ricky called from down the path. That was my cue to leave.

"Well, it's been real," I said with a little soldier salute. "See ya around, Elmo."

Eric hated being called Elmo—the initials for Eric Lewis

Mulvaney Ortiz. That's why I called him that. A lot.

He did a little chin raise movement and with that I was dismissed. His swarm of friends enveloped him in their nonsense, and he went back to easy smiles, like he didn't have a care in the world. It was a thin façade, but no one else seemed aware of it.

As I walked toward the backyard fence, I shook off our conversation, but I was left with a distinct feeling someone was watching me. I looked over my shoulder as I swung the gate open, and although other people were talking to him, Eric was still staring at me. It was strange, but this whole night had been weird, so I let it go.

Turns out, that was a mistake. One of many to come.

CHAPTER TWO

Kelsie's Log of Failure

DAY THIRTY OF NO CONTACT

Kelsie Miller's Phone

Bri Bri Hoffman

> I ran into Elmo at a party. Remember the last time we ran into him outside of school? Lolol. Anyhow, he was asking about you. I wish I knew how you were. Do you hate Seattle and desperately want to come back yet?? I wish you'd been at the party—it's not the same without you. Nothing is. I miss you

CHAPTER THREE

Before Everything Went Wrong

DECEMBER OF LAST YEAR

Bri showed up at my door about fifteen minutes late (so, right on time by the standard Bri curve). Light-up reindeer antlers decorated her blond head.

"We wish you a Merry Christmas," she sang, pitch-perfect as always.

"Why, thank you." I laughed after she finished the song. Bri was Jewish, but she loved Christmas music.

"You ready?" she asked.

"Wait." I put on a Ho, Ho, Ho headband. "Okay, now I'm ready."

"Oh, the irony." She flicked one of the Hos.

I snorted. I'd just been called a prude at the last party she and Teagan had dragged me to. They'd defended me saying I wasn't a prude; it was just that all the boys there were ugly. Both were kind of true.

"Is that Bri?" my mom yelled from inside.

"Yeah, Mom," I said. "We're heading to Gladsmith's, remember?"

"Oh, right, the Victorian Streetwalk is tonight," Mom said. She appeared next to me in the doorway and wrapped Bri in a hug. Bri leaned into my mom, who'd been like her second mom all her life and for the past two and a half years had been closer than her real mom, who'd up and moved away. "It's nice of you girls to help out."

"All Kel's idea," Bri said with a smile.

It was. We'd been hanging out at Teagan's bakery, and as always Teagan had been scheming expansion ideas for her family's business. Brianna was the one with CEO goals, but Teagan had a head for numbers and dreamed of making her parents' bakery a "global brand." I wasn't sure how she was going to do that as a future engineer, but if anyone could do both, it was Teagan. She managed to be captain of the Carver track team and soccer team, play in a band, and work at the bakery.

Plus, her parents' baked goods were tasty enough to go worldwide. While doing homework and eating still-warm chocolate croissants, I'd mentioned that it was a shame the café would be closed for the Victorian Streetwalk—the town tradition that kicked off the holiday season.

"You guys should stay open and sell holiday treats," I'd said. "Sop up some of the hot toddy liquor."

"You're a genius," Teagan had said.

"Well, we all already know that." Bri had elbowed me and grinned.

Teagan had jumped out of her seat. "No, let's do it. I'll run it by my parents, but we could sell holiday-themed stuff to the drunk tourists wandering around and make a killing."

The rest was history. Teagan's parents okayed staying open until nine, as long as we provided the labor and her older brother, Mack, supervised. Bri was happy with that since she was always talking about how hot Mack was. Objectively he was cute, just not my type. I didn't have a type. But I loved the arrangement because it included all the free baked goods I could eat.

So Bri picked me up that afternoon. It was maybe forty-five degrees out and getting colder, but Bri had the top down on her convertible. She took any non-raining or -snowing opportunity to have the roof off the Audi, and I couldn't blame her. I would've done the same if I'd had a car. We drove with the heat and stereo blasting the few blocks to Broadway, the town's main drag.

I put my mitten-covered hands in the air as I danced in the passenger seat to one of my favorite songs. Bri nodded her head along to the beat. Guys whistled at us as we pulled into downtown and we laughed at them. It was one of those moments you'd want to stay in forever. But within minutes we pulled into the parking lot and walked over to Gladsmith's, the bakery café.

"Hey! Thanks again for helping out," Teagan said, coming around the counter. Her warm brown skin had a dusting of glitter and powdered sugar on it. She air-kissed Bri, then leaned down to do the same to me. I stood on my tiptoes to make up some of our ten-inch height difference.

At first I hadn't liked Teagan. At all. It was nothing against her personally. I was just jealous of her . . . for, like, two years. We met freshman year at Carver, and she and Bri had hit it off right away. Bri sang and Teagan played guitar, so they had an instant music connection. They both liked obscure bands and they also were on the soccer team together. Add that they both had an effortlessly chic thing going on and me . . . not so much. I was petite and strange, which my dad tried to pass off as "unique," which was simply code for "weird." If I made enough money at some point, I could be labeled "eccentric," but now . . . just strange.

By the start of junior year I'd started to like Teagan too, although Bri was still the linchpin of the group. When Teagan and I were alone, there was always an off silence, like a piano missing a key.

That day, though, it was my idea for the three of us to hang out. We shucked off our coats and sold a ton of baked goods and cocoa to families and somewhat sober couples enjoying the festivities. With every sale I was a little prouder of my idea. I refilled the nearly empty cookie case with more gingerbread men and Saratoga sugar-cookie reindeer—horses with antlers, which were also my idea.

When I stood up, there was Eric in front of me. All six feet plus of him. Only he was dressed like a Victorian gentleman complete with a top hat on his brown head. I couldn't help it. I laughed right in his face.

I covered my mouth with my hand. "My apologies."

"What are you doing here?" he asked.

"I could ask you the same." I managed to suppress another laugh. "Nice threads, Elmo."

"It really is a nice costume," Teagan said, coming up next to me all heart eyes. She leaned forward on the case toward him and batted her long lashes. I wasn't sure if she was kidding around or actually flirting. Probably both.

Eric gave her one of his million-dollar smiles. And I groaned from my toes to my throat.

"Thanks, Teagan." He dropped his grin and looked over at me. "To answer your question, Miller: My dads are in the charity caroling group and their baritone came down with laryngitis so I got roped into singing tonight. And wearing this."

"Well, you make it look good," Teagan added.

I side-eyed her. Shameless.

Brianna came out of the kitchen with a tray of miniature holiday cakes Mack had made. She was still looking back at Teagan's handsome brother as she swung through the door. Then she stopped in her tracks, her eyes going wide.

"Eric. Hey," she said. "You look . . ."

"Like a *Great Expectations* cosplay?" I offered. "A Dickens-verse fanboy? Heathcliff's misery?"

"Nice headband," Eric sniped.

Heat rushed into my face. God, I hated my blush. I wanted to rip off the headband and toss it in the trash, but I wouldn't give him the satisfaction.

"You're both festive." Bri sounded like a mom tired from dealing with two bickering toddlers, which wasn't fair since he'd started it.

Eric adjusted the lapels of his coat. "Thanks, Bri. Just came in to warm up with some cocoa. I'll take a dozen of those little cakes back too. They look too good to pass up."

Sure, fifty dollars in cakes, just like that.

"You know you can have anything you want," Teagan said, lowering her voice and her eyelids.

Oh, come on.

I rolled my eyes and walked toward the kitchen. Better to see if Mack needed a hand decorating cakes or wiping down counters or scrubbing toilets. Anything was better than the nausea of watching Eric and his fan club.

"I'll text you later about the AP English assignment," Eric called after me. We were unfortunately paired together on a school project. Yet again.

"Can't wait!" I said.

"Great to see you as always, Miller."

"At least it was good for one of us," I said, tossing my hair over my shoulder.

I slammed through the swinging door to the industrial kitchen and threw off my headband.

"Easy, Kelly. Don't Hulk through our door," Mack said. He smiled with his dimples showing. He knew my name but called me Kelly, which was nice for some reason. He was two years older than us and going to community college while working as a baker.

"Elmo came in," I said, hoisting myself up to sit on a counter. I folded my arms and pouted. His presence just . . . unnerved me.

"Ah, the nemesis," Mack laughed. "Come help with the Saratoga reindeer."

I hopped down and grabbed the frosting bags. I wasn't a cook by any means, but I was good at art, and decorating cookies was just another medium. Painting was my favorite.

I piped the brown frosting on; it was nice to focus on something other than firing shots at Eric.

"Hey." Mack bumped his hip into me. "Why you gotta show me up and make them better than mine?"

I smiled just as Bri sauntered into the kitchen. Was it just me or had she reapplied lipstick?

"All clear," she said.

"Good," I said.

Bri raised an eyebrow at me. "You could've been a little nicer, you know. You're not in school. You don't always have to be an asshole to him."

I squinted one eye. "Could I have been nicer, though? He's insufferable."

"Insufferably hot," Teagan said, swinging around the door-frame.

"Ew," Mack and I said at the same time.

Chimes went off, meaning another customer had come

in. Bri laughed, shaking her head, and walked out to serve them.

"Y'all should just bang and get it over with," Teagan said.

I widened my eyes and pointed to my chest as she stared at me. "Who?" I said. "Me? And . . . Eric?"

"Yup," Teagan said.

I mimed a puking motion. "No thanks. I'd rather bang your bread mixer."

"Hot," Mack said with a wink.

"Ew," Teagan said. "Come on, Kel. I'll save you from my suddenly pervy brother."

She and I laughed as she pulled me by my hand out of the kitchen. Teagan, Bri, and I sailed through the rest of the Streetwalk, serving a ton of customers. When it got quiet around dinnertime, I started a competition of who could lure in the most customers from the street. Bri won by serenading people in like a Christmas siren.

After we split up the generous tips and closed down the shop, we went back to Bri's and jammed in her dad's basement. Midlife Crisis poster boy David Hoffman had a full band setup and even a stage down there. So we played to our usual audience of Bri's favorite ratty stuffed animal, Mr. Lionheart. I smacked the tambourine, which any monkey could do, but Bri and Teagan wanted me to feel included despite my lack of musical talent.

Once we finished a set of songs, and the rest of the red velvet cake from the bakery, we fell asleep on the couches. Bri hugged her lion/bear/pig thing on the love seat while Teagan and I slept feet to shoulders on the longer sectional.

Another perfect Saturday night in the books. And one of many I'd hoped for in senior year. Instead, I'd lost everything faster than a sugar crash.

CHAPTER FOUR

On Sunday morning I was still in my pajamas, brushing my teeth and minding my own damn business, when someone rang our doorbell.

It was ten o'clock so I figured it was just a delivery or Jehovah's Witness or something. Anyhow, that's why I answered the door braless, biting on a toothbrush and wearing sleep shorts with a Moana T-shirt.

Hanna, my little sister, thought I looked like Moana, which wasn't true. If anything, I looked like Mulan. Hanna was just like the three little rambunctious princes from *Brave*, and we'd exchanged character shirts last Christmas. But back to my nemesis standing stunned across from me with two huge coffees in his hands.

Caught off guard, I slammed the door in his face. Then I took a breath, gathered myself, and opened it again.

I shook my head with a question of "why are you even

here," then raised my finger—the universal sign for "wait a second"—and left him at the door. I raced upstairs to the bathroom and rinsed my mouth out. I tossed on jeans and a tank (including a bra) and cleaned the crud out of my eyes. Anything more would've looked like I was trying and that was way beside the point.

At least it was better than being seen in a Victorian costume.

As I walked down the stairs to my front door, I couldn't imagine why Eric was at my house. He'd been to my place plenty of times, but for parties when my mom made me invite the whole class and mandatory things like school projects. We'd get paired together often because we both had last names that started with *M*. He could've just gone by Ortiz, or Ortiz Mulvaney, but no, it had to be Mulvaney Ortiz, and since I was Miller, more often than not we sat near each other.

And now he was in my doorway after I just saw him last night. Lucky me.

I gripped the edge of the wooden door. "What are you doing here?"

"Good morning to you, too," he said.

I let out a loud "ugh" as my nails dug into the wood. Eric and his formalities.

I did a little bow. "Top of the morning, my good sir. 'Tis a pleasant morn. What errand hath arisen for you to grace my threshold?"

He stared for a second then extended an enormous iced coffee at me.

"Um, thanks?" My voice rose at the end like a question.

"Can you talk for a minute?" He pointed to the Adirondack chairs on my front porch.

I shrugged, utterly confused, but closed the door behind me. I followed him because I was extremely curious, and what else did I have going on? Even my little sister had commented that I was home too much. Sick burn from an eight-year-old.

My house was an old, but cool bungalow with a deep porch. Unlike Eric's parents, mine never could've afforded to buy a house in pricey downtown Saratoga Springs, but this one was left to them years ago by my dad's great-aunt. My life's goal was to one day be a wealthy cat lady like Aunt Helen.

Eric and I sat on the deck chairs, and he put his coffee on the side table. He silently fidgeted, staring at nothing while rubbing his hands on his shorts. As always, he didn't have a wrinkle on him.

In the odd silence, I yawned, then took a sip of the large Dunkin' coffee. It was hazelnut vanilla with cream and liquid sugar. Just how I liked it—actually, it was exactly the way I ordered it down to the pump sugar instead of crystals.

"How'd you know what I drink?" I said, glancing at the ordering label.

"You've brought one in every day since middle school," he said.

It was true. I'd never been a morning person and middle

school was medieval-torture early, so I'd started drinking coffee. I still thought I might've been a morning person on Korea time, but as I was hurled into Eastern Standard when I was adopted as a baby . . . no such luck.

"What do you want, Eric?" I asked after more silence.

"I want my life back." He stared over at me, his eyes as intense as I'd ever seen them.

I raised an eyebrow. "Did you bargain it away to a sea witch?"

"Be normal for a second," he said.

"Easier said than done," I murmured.

"I can't stop thinking about what you said last night," he continued.

"And that was . . ." I gestured for him to elaborate. I couldn't remember anything I'd mentioned at the party that would've kept him thinking for twelve hours.

"That we should go to UPenn," he said.

I waited for him to crack a smile or wink or something to tell me he was kidding. But no. He was serious.

"Eric, I know you're not familiar with them, but that was a ha-ha joke. A funny. I wasn't serious. It wasn't a real suggestion." I took another sip of my sugary, perfect coffee and watched neighbors go by with their seven-hundred-dollar strollers and adopt-don't-shop righteous dogs.

"But it could be," he said.

He had that same determined look as when he ran with a project. When he was winning a debate as team captain. When he convinced nearly all five hundred students at Carver to pitch in for a park cleanup. When he beat me by five votes for fifth-grade class president. Eric was ambition incarnate—razor sharp and almost always successful, aside from some football losses. But he couldn't think we should show up at UPenn. This had to be a trap.

"Hilarious," I said.

"I'm serious, Miller." He leaned forward, nearly touching me. I moved backward in my large seat. "I need to see Jessica. I know what we have between us and I'm certain if she sees me . . ." He trailed off into his own thoughts and then refocused on me. "And you know Brianna better than anyone. Don't you want to see her again?"

I blinked a few times. He hit on the thing I wanted most in the world. I hated that she moved across the country to be with her mother. Her mom had never been there for her—I was more like family to her. Yet Brianna chose to leave everything behind, including me and her dad, the moment Elaine Taylor (formerly Hoffman) had offered to send for her. And now I wasn't sure if I'd ever see her again.

"I . . . of course I do . . . but—" I stammered.

"We could make this happen," he said. "I looked at Bri's posts, and she's flying into Philadelphia Wednesday night—three days from now. I have a game on Friday, and practice the days before, but I could skip Thursday and we could head down there. It's four and a half hours by car. If we leave Thursday morning, that'll give us a whole day to try to find them and patch things up. Then we'll drive back at night."

I admit, it was tempting. I started getting swept up in Eric's fervor. We'd go there. I'd see Bri across the campus lawn and we'd smile and everything would be okay. We'd go on the tour together, just the two of us. Plus Eric.

Wait.

Eric.

We? Us? Nine hours in the car together? It might sound (definitely was) petty, but the last time I'd trusted him, he pushed me off the balance beam in gym class in second grade. Everyone had laughed when I face-planted onto the blue mats. Well, everyone but me and him. I'd blinked back tears to find Eric smirking at me. And right then I knew: we'd never be friends.

For the rest of our lives, he'd confirmed my decision.

I glanced to the side like I was staring into a camera of that old show my dad loved, *The Office*. It was the one that made him want to be a screenwriter, and we'd watched it together like a million times.

But as I looked back at Eric, he still seemed so sincere. I didn't know what had gotten into him, but this plan was ludicrous and totally unlike him.

"We can't just show up on campus for no reason." I stood to go back into my house. "Thanks for the coffee and the Sunday morning weirdness, but honestly, you should let this go."

He stood up. "Can you?"

"Can I what?"

"Can you just let Bri go?" He stared down at me, his expression both pained and hopeful.

Of course I couldn't. I'd let Teagan go. We were friends through Bri, and once our connector was gone, we were bound to go our separate ways. She had her cool girl-band friends and soccer teammates and I had . . . well, nothing. But I'd figured we'd lose touch in college, so it was just an early departure—or at least that's what I told myself.

But Bri? No.

Despite her completely ignoring me, I still messaged her every day. I remained ever optimistic she'd talk to me again, since she hadn't blocked me, even on Day 31. But what he was proposing—physically showing up there—that was the realm of Netflix stalkers and restraining orders. Who would even do that? People who'd been cut off and were desperate. Admittedly, we fit the bill. Our lives were so out of whack, we were hanging out together. But how could we actually go there?

"It's a day," he said, probably sensing my hesitation. "One day and we could get our lives back on track. You fix whatever happened with Bri. I fix things with Jessica. We come back conquering heroes."

I allowed myself to return to the dream of it working out. Of smiling at Bri across a campus lawn and her realizing I made a huge effort to find her at UPenn. We'd be best friends again—even if she'd still live in Seattle for a year. After that we'd be much closer once she went to her dream school and I went . . . somewhere (TBD). But a dream wasn't reality. And there was a vague feeling inside me that it would not be as easy as seeing Bri across a lawn. Something awful had to have happened for her to end our twelve-year friendship. Only, what the hell was it? All I wanted was an answer, and a trip to UPenn might provide it. Still, I shook my head.

"How do you think this'll even work? What would we do?" I said.

"We're the smartest kids at Carver . . . ," he began.

I mean, he was right. The only reason we didn't have perfect GPAs in our hypercompetitive school was because we'd both had Mr. Jones for AP English. And Mr. Jones didn't believe in one hundreds, because "no one is perfect"—aka "I am a total dick of a teacher."

Eric took a sip of his coffee. "We'll figure it out."

"We'll figure it out? That's it? That's literally your plan? I'm not enjoying this role reversal," I said.

I was the one who usually figured things would somehow work out, like with the Victorian Streetwalk. I came up with an idea and let the rest fall into place, ad libbing as I needed to. Eric laid out his plans in painstaking detail. The kid put all his clothes, down to his socks, out the night before school, which I'd stumbled on while we were doing a project together. So what was this shit?

"We'll come up with something," he said. "We have three days. You don't have to give me an answer right now, but this is our chance. Say you'll at least think about it?"

His hazel eyes pleaded with me, and on a lesser person, the puppy dog eyes would've worked. I opened my mouth and gestured, stirring the air with my hands. I was about to say no when my parents' old Subaru rattled into the driveway. Reflexively, Eric and I jumped apart like we'd been tonguing each other on the porch.

My parents and Hanna got out of the car all smiles. She must've coerced them into getting her McDonald's breakfast, because she looked particularly smug and my dad had a McCafé iced coffee in his hand.

"Well, if it isn't Eric!" my mom said.

As class mom on and off through elementary school, she knew Eric well. Plus, Dr. Ortiz was our family physician and our parents were friends through some Facebook group, because small towns were forsaken by the gods.

She came up the porch steps and gave him a mom hug. Such a frigging traitor.

"Good morning, Mrs. Miller, Mr. Miller. Have you all been having a good summer?" Eric asked.

The offensive part was this wasn't even a front he put on for parents. He actually wanted to know.

"We have," my dad said, shaking his hand. Even my dad, who wasn't a total turncoat, liked him. "We brought you a coffee, hon, but I see someone else beat us to it."

"Can never have too much," I said. It was a lie. I'd had too much coffee and jittered my way around Carver totally paranoid and able to see time, but I took the second coffee and stood there with two. I wanted my family inside and Eric gone. Stat.

"Has he been here all morning?" Hanna asked. My little sister was eight. She was missing two front teeth and one soul.

Heat spread up my face like a brushfire. My accursed cheeks were probably as red as Hanna's hair.

"Just got here a few minutes ago, Little Miller." Eric bent down and gave her a fist bump. With a satisfied, gap-toothed smile, she disappeared into the house. An ominous sounding crash later, my dad excused himself and went in after her.

"I dropped by to see if Kelsie wanted to come with me on a University of Pennsylvania campus tour this week," Eric said to my mom. "My dads would feel better if I had company for the drive, and I remembered she told the college advisor she was planning to apply to all the Ivies."

I stared at him, pursing my lips. I hated Eric Mulvaney Ortiz and his steel trap memory. It was why he'd beaten me for debate team captain.

"Oh, that's a great idea. Fall semester already started there, right?" my mom said.

"Yes, ma'am," Eric said.

I tilted my head. It must've been hard for him to talk and kiss that much ass at the same time.

"You both could get a good sense of campus life," she said. "But don't you have your heart set on Hopkins, Eric?"

"I do, but it's probably best to see other colleges too," he replied.

According to the degrees on his walls, Dr. Ortiz had gone to Johns Hopkins for undergraduate and med school. Eric had every intention of following in his doctor dad's footsteps. He'd never considered anywhere else even though his architect dad had gone to Cooper Union, another great school in the heart of Manhattan. Cooper was on the top of my list, but it had only three types of programs: art, architecture, and engineering. I might've been able to wedge myself into one of those categories, but the problem was, I had no idea what I wanted to be when I grew up. I didn't understand how anyone our age did. Still, the huge selling point of Cooper was that it was free. Money had been super tight since my dad left his full-time job to pursue screenwriting a few years back. He'd make it one day—I was sure of it, but in the meantime, there wasn't anything in the budget for college.

Eric had no such worries.

"Do you want to come inside?" Mom asked.

I stared at her. It was a blatant example of teenager abuse.

"He was just leaving," I said.

Mom glared at me like I'd spoken out of turn. I had. But still.

"No, I should be going," he said. "Dads and I need to make some paella for the soup kitchen."

Of course.

Mom was all heart eyes. "You should take Kelsie with you sometime."

Ugh. I folded my arms. I should've called the cops when she invited him in.

"She's always welcome," he said. I shook my head a little to indicate my rising homicidal urge. "But we're all set for today," he added.

"Well, stop by anytime," Mom said. "Don't be a stranger."

I widened my eyes and stared at her. That settled it. I would not be the one taking care of her when she got old. She'd have to rely on the little gremlin for all her elderly needs.

Mom smirked before heading into the house. Unbelievable. Moms were The Worst. Eric was lucky to have two dads.

"Great visit!" I said once my mom closed the door.

"Just . . . think about it. Please?" he said.

He looked at me like I contained all the hope in the world. But his latest ass-kissing had only reminded me of how very different we were. How Eric always got what he wanted. And with things uncertain with Bri, I was in no mood to go on a long road trip just to help my nemesis get his happily ever after with the perfect girl.

"Thought about it and no," I said. "I'll stick to being a web stalker and not a real one. You have fun feeding your paella to the homeless, Saint Elmo."

With that last jab in, I headed for the door. I tried to turn the knob, but because I had two cups in my hands, I spilled ice-cold coffee all over my chest. Before Eric could try to help, I got the door open and slammed it shut behind me.

I stood there dripping Dunkin' on the woven floor mat with my whole family staring at me. Banner start to the day, but I did know one thing: I was not going to UPenn with Eric.

CHAPTER FIVE

Kelsie Miller's Phone
Hell-mo Eric

Have you given any more thought to the trip?

Yes

And?

For the fourth time: no. Why are you so hot for me coming with you anyhow?

Idk. It seems less desperate with company. And you're in the same boat as me

Oh, it's desperate either way. Bring one of your football bros if you need company

Look, you're the smartest girl I know

Smartest person you know

Whatever. You know what I mean

Have you actually won debates like this?

You think differently from me and I may need ideas to win Jessica back. And you may need ideas with Bri. I can help. We can work together—we always win as a team. And once we succeed, we never have to talk about this again

That's the best argument you've made so far—that you'll leave me alone

Is that a yes?

No

CHAPTER SIX

By Wednesday afternoon, I caved.

For the record: I did not cave because of Eric's arguments or constant harassment. No, it was all because of Bri. And Teagan.

My ex-best friend flew out to the East Coast as scheduled on Wednesday and posted an airport layover selfie on Instagram. As usual, she looked perfect—blond hair in natural waves, aviator sunglasses, dusting of freckles on her nose. She had on a comfortable yet stylish outfit as she sipped her usual Starbucks iced macchiato and the reflection of a plane taking off showed in her glasses. The post was captioned with some kind of "flying toward the future" nonsense. It would've been corny from someone else, but Bri was just Bri. Never fake or trying too hard. She said things because she meant them, and people always liked her for it.

Teagan and Bri had rapid-fire commented under her IG

post, while completely ignoring my reply about how I hoped she had a good trip. As I read their back-and-forth, I realized the two of them had a new inside joke, something about a plum, and it broke my heart. Bri and I were normally the ones with inside jokes. We'd met when she'd bounded into the seat next to me on the first day of kindergarten, and we'd become instant best friends. There were too many shared memories to count—innumerable playdates, going out on her family's boat, trying soccer because it was Bri's favorite sport, and her trying out dancing school with me. We could exchange one glance and laugh ourselves to tears remembering a moment from the cafeteria in fourth grade, but now, not only had I been replaced in Bri's world, I didn't even speak the language anymore.

Right at that moment, when the fissure in my heart became a ravine, Eric had asked me again to go to UPenn. This time I said yes.

I kept telling myself it would be one day—for better or worse.

At dinner, as we passed around my dad's famous (only to him) enchiladas, and after Dad bounced his latest film pitch off me, I told my parents I'd decided to tour UPenn with Eric. They, of course, were cool with it. That was the one advantage to Eric being Eric: parents loved him.

While we cleaned up, Eric texted me details for the next morning. I didn't reply, preferring to wash dishes and brainstorm comparison titles with my dad.

After some family movie time, I was lying on top of my bed

reading when Hanna came crashing into my room. She had our cat, Snuggles, in a light headlock. For some reason, the white cat, who was a known serial killer and likely Jack the Ripper in a previous life, absolutely adored Hanna. I didn't get why. She was cute but also a disaster of loose teeth, chocolate stains, and grand larceny.

"You can look, but don't touch anything," I said, barely glancing up from *Opposite of Always*.

"Why?" she whined, halfway to my closet.

"Because you just had a Popsicle. You're practically a glue trap," I said. I made a mental note to lock my bedroom door before I left to keep my worldly possessions safe.

"I just wanted to look at your clothes," she huffed. "I wasn't going to touch."

Lies.

"By 'look' you mean steal some," I said.

It was both adorable and impossible that Hanna loved wearing my stuff. A few years back she'd even wanted to dye her hair black like mine. I didn't have the heart to tell her she still wouldn't have looked Korean, but the sweetness of it almost made up for the constant thievery.

Almost.

Admittedly, I had a soft spot for Hanna. I'd loved her since she was a tuft of red hair and endless cries. I was nine when she was born, so even though we were siblings, it wasn't like Teagan and her brother, Mack, who were two years apart. I was more Hanna's minimom.

Real Mom appeared in the doorway frowning at how Snuggles was letting Hanna handle him. Mom had brown hair, and my dad did as well. Where the red came from was anyone's guess. Satan was my hypothesis.

"Hanna, baby, go wash your hands and brush your teeth," Mom said. "And wipe off Snuggles. You got some cherry Popsicle on him."

I smirked at being proven right yet again.

Hanna made some aggrieved noise, but she did as she was told. Mom wandered farther into my bedroom.

She straightened things out on my dresser. "So, you're leaving at what time tomorrow?"

"I negotiated for nine," I said.

Originally, Eric had wanted to leave at seven in the goddamn morning. I threatened to pull out of the trip right then, and we compromised.

"Okay," Mom said. "And you'll be back when?"

"Not sure. We're going to stop for lunch and dinner and it depends on how the tours and everything go, plus Jersey traffic. Probably late, but I'll text when we leave."

It was a weird question since I'd just told her all of that in the kitchen.

"Well, you know you have to be safe at UPenn, right?" Mom said.

I looked up from my book and put it aside. Mom was all about safety. She was literally the safety manager at a plant. But she wasn't looking me in the eye when she asked. Instead, she was deeply focused on putting books back into my bookcase. In retrospect, I should've seen the warning sign of where the conversation was headed.

"Well, I was planning on eating unwrapped candy and wearing all black while jogging with traffic at night," I said. "I guess I need to rethink my strategy now."

She tilted her head. "I'm serious, Kel. Eric is a good kid, but you know to use protection if it goes there."

I gagged then screamed. "Mother! Ugh! No. No. No, I don't know that, nor will I think about that. His personality is birth control enough. Why would you even let me go on this trip if you thought I'd do that?"

In response, she shrugged. Shrugged!

"Well, you're seventeen and you'll be in college soon and—" she began.

"Get out of my room right now with this hippie cool mom bullshit." I pointed to my doorway.

"Language," she warned.

"Sorry, new age cool mom bullshit."

"Kelsie Marie." Mom lifted one finger and one eyebrow, the well-known sign for "that's far enough." Mom hated bad language, and she had to deal with the fact that Hanna would repeat everything like a damaged little parrot.

I pursed my lips. "No, Mom. No plans on banging Eric in his car on the side of the road, thanks. But, hey, if you're going to the store, pick me up a value pack of condoms in case I want to take down the UPenn rugby team while I'm there. On a tour. During the middle of the day."

Honestly.

She drew a long, steadying breath before turning toward the door. "The worst thing you picked up from your dad was this sense of humor." She gestured up and down but was trying not to laugh.

Mom was right. I one hundred percent got my humor from my dad. And one day his comedy would make us rich when he became a successful screenwriter. I just knew it.

"You love us!" I called after her.

She paused in the doorway. "I do. And I'm serious about being safe."

I threw a pair of slippers at her and just missed as the door shut.

Sex.

I shook my head and sighed. Everything always seemed to be about sex. Movies, TV, definitely Carver, and grossly my mom's mind went there. And . . . sex just wasn't something I was interested in. Not really.

Trying to go with the flow, I'd kissed two boys and a girl and just felt . . . nothing. The closest I'd come to feeling any kind of spark was with Ryan Culligan. We'd been close friends all through middle school, and I'd been happy when he also made it into Carver. During freshman year, though, I suddenly found myself thinking about him as something other than a friend. We were working on an electricity project together and our faces got close and I wanted him to kiss me. I held my pillow at night and thought about Ryan. I'd known him four years or so, and I'd started feeling the attraction my friends described from glancing at a hot person at a party, but nothing ever came of it because Ryan moved to Louisville the summer before sophomore year.

So, yes, my romantic experience was limited to a glance over a circuit. Hot times.

Bri and Teagan tried to understand. Teagan was kind of a flirt and didn't really get it. But Bri thought I might be aromantic or demisexual, neither of which I understood. Especially demisexual. I'd looked up the definition and it seemed to fit everyone. Didn't everyone need an emotional connection to someone to want them? Still, my friends never made me feel weird about it. I was safe in my trio.

All I'd wanted was one more year of normalcy. One where I could put the massive decisions of becoming an adult on hold. I wanted to eat more pastries at Gladsmith's and jam in Bri's basement or study on her dock on Saratoga Lake as her super-sweet dad tried way too hard to connect with us.

As I went to bed, I clung to the hope that Eric was right—we could both fix our lives the next day.

It was the first time in my life I wanted Eric to be right about anything.

It was the first time he'd be wrong.

CHAPTER SEVEN

Kelsie's Log of Failure

DAY THIRTY-FIVE OF NO CONTACT

To Brianna (BB_Hoff@gmailplus.com)

8:40 a.m.

Bri Bri,

Hey! Look, I get that you're not talking to me, but I miss the hell out of you. I wish you'd tell me what I did to make you stop responding to me. I wish I could take whatever it is back.

But I wanted to tell you that Dad found out today that he's short-listed for the Light Project!!! The contest you told him about months ago. He's trying to downplay his chances, but I'm so stoked for him. It could really change everything for us. Please write back and let me know what's going on with you. I saw that you're going to UPenn. Is it still your #1?

Love ya.

CHAPTER EIGHT

I wasn't in Eric's car for more than thirty seconds before I started rethinking the whole trip.

For one, my dad had found out that morning that he'd made it to the last stage of a really big screenwriting competition. We'd all jumped up and down in the kitchen for, like, fifteen minutes after he got the email. Sounds excessive, but he'd made it to the top ten out of thousands of entries. It'd been amazing to see the joy and pride on his face when we finally sat down and he tried to play it cool after so many rejections. This was real, concrete proof of his talent, and I wasn't sure about leaving right after his good news. But he'd told me to go because it would still be a while before we heard anything else.

As I got in Eric's car, though, I realized I'd forgotten a key negative: Eric was a goddamn morning person. He was all energy and good cheer as I crashed into the passenger seat. His dads had bought the BMW for him as soon as he'd turned sixteen, and he'd kept it in pristine condition for the past two years. Was I jealous? Yes. Was he way too privileged? Also yes.

The last thing irking me was we still didn't have a real plan for UPenn. The one and only concrete step we'd agreed to was: find our exes. He didn't like my ideas of skywriting or residence hall bomb threats, and his idea of enlisting the help of the registrar and admissions office put me to sleep. He'd booked an afternoon campus tour for us, but that was all we had to go on. And while we'd have four and a half painful hours to brainstorm together, that wasn't a selling point.

"What? You're not having second thoughts, are you?" Eric said as he reversed down my driveway.

"Did I say something?" I asked.

"You're making a face," he replied.

I immediately reset my expression back to neutral. "That's just my face."

"It isn't though," he murmured.

"I'm fine. Let's do it." I wasn't fine, of course, but no backing out now. I'd never be able to explain the change of heart to my parents.

Eric started directions to the UPenn campus. The robot lady voice barked out the route we already knew to the highway. We drove in the opposite direction of the horse track, away from all the gambling summer tourists whose money made the town run.

As we passed the stores and restaurants of downtown

Saratoga, I kept thinking about how I wanted to get out of this town and experience somewhere new. It had always been in my head, to go away to college, but Bri friend-dumping me had made leaving a priority. I wasn't sure which school, but a big city where everyone didn't know each other's business all the time would've been a welcome change.

And a place where there weren't so many memories.

We stopped at a light, and on the left was Congress Park, the place where one lazy day in middle school, I'd let my guard down and given Eric a chance, only to have him say things that my petty heart had never forgiven.

The light changed and we moved past it. I wished it would've been that easy for me to let go.

"So, um, how was your summer?" Eric asked.

I stared over at him.

He cleared his throat. "I mean, aside from Bri and all that."

"We don't have to do the small talk thing," I said. "Really, it's fine."

"Noted."

He hit the button for XM Radio, and the music was a welcome distraction as we drove down the less congested part of town. I had memories in all those places too, although better ones: treating the red gremlin to McDonald's after her first day of kindergarten; going to sushi with Bri and her first girl-friend, Leila, sophomore year; trying and failing to keep up with Teagan after she'd talked me into going for a "jog" with her in the state park last winter.

But Eric caressing the dashboard phone holder shook me out of the past.

"What's going on there?" I said.

He looked confused, and I pointed to his intimate relationship with a cell phone device.

"Oh, Jessica got it for me." He dropped his hand onto the wheel. "I used to keep my phone on my lap or in the cup holder, you know? But she wanted me to be safe while I was driving. It was a really nice gift and so like her to think of it."

At a total loss for what to say, I nodded and the conversation dropped.

Eric had gone to Dunkin' before picking me up, and he'd gotten me my iced coffee again. Next to it was his black coffee. That's right—no milk or sugar, just serial killer hot black coffee. I grabbed mine and took a long pull, trying to shake the fact that I was anxious. Getting our exes back wasn't an area where book smarts were useful. Aside from academics, Eric had football knowledge and I was good (not great) at art, but neither of those talents was going to help.

We were screwed. But we had to at least try.

I rubbed my face and caught him looking over as he merged onto the highway. One song later, I saw him do it again.

"Creeeeeeper," I said, trying my best to sound possessed.

He gave me an unamused side-eye. "I'm trying to figure out how to phrase this."

"Since when have you ever been at a loss for words?" I said.

Eric was the kind of person who texted paragraphs when

we were working on school projects together. They should've come with ominous scores because they were villain monologues. I swore he won debates simply by outtalking his opponents.

He uttered a guttural noise. "What's up with you and Brianna?"

I tilted my head. "Huh?"

"Oratory fireworks, Miller." He finally took a sip of his coffee. Now that we were on the highway, his fancy car could basically go on autopilot between the cruise control, lane assist, and blind spot blinky lights.

"What are you inquiring about?" I asked, hitting all the syllables of inquiring. "It's like I told you on Saturday, she stopped talking to me once she moved to Seattle."

"I remember, but . . . well, yeah, I'll just ask the question," he said. "Are you in love with her?"

I nearly spit out my drink. To prevent myself from spraying coffee across the pristine dash, I closed my lips at the last second and inhaled/choked on it instead. Bad decision. I coughed again and again and couldn't clear my coffee-soggy windpipe. My sinuses were aflame and my eyes teared.

Eric passed me a napkin from the center console. I snatched it out of his hand and wiped my face before blowing hazelnut flavoring out my nose. I bet Jessica, if she was real, had never choked on a beverage in her life. Given Eric's concerned stare, no girl in his orbit ever had.

I wadded up my napkin and tossed it to the custom floor

mats with more force than necessary. He frowned.

"There's a trash bag right here," he said. It was hanging off the gearshift. Because of course there was an in-car trash receptacle. Everything had to be perfect and tidy in his universe. For example, his car didn't have a speck of dust on it. It was totally different from my parents' Subaru, where, because of Hanna, dust was the least of our worries. Bri had also gotten her convertible when she turned sixteen, but hers was littered with clothes, papers, and soccer gear. Definitely not crime scene scrubbed like this.

And Eric had just asked if I was in love with her.

"Honestly, what the hell?" I said.

"Well, you're so obsessed with getting her back," he said. "I thought maybe there was more going on than just friends and maybe you needed to talk to someone about it. That's all."

As his words sank in, the rage of fifty pissed-off vipers reared up in me—not because he thought I was gay, but because in order to want her back, I had to be in love with her? It felt like the snakes were actually hissing in my head. For a split second I considered holding back, but why?

"Seriously?" I said. "'Just friends'? Wanting to kiss her would make this all more legit? More justifiable? She's my best friend. She's been my best friend since we were five. Or . . . she was." I paused. I hated having to correct myself to the past tense. "We had a dozen years together, she was like a sister to me, and now she's just gone. There's an impossible emptiness to fill. I love her through and through, but no, I'm not in love with her."

And I did love her. All of her. I loved the way she really listened to a person's problems. The spacey but sometimes laser-focused way she glided through life. How I knew to add fifteen minutes to her arrival times, because try as she might, inevitably she was late and sincerely sorry for it. Yet somehow she was always on the cutting edge of music, fashion, anything pop culture. She was someone you just wanted to be around, but who didn't get caught up in gossip or the pettiness of being naturally popular. She was funny, but also kind. Generous, but not for show or praise. She was forgetful and messy, but genuine. She was competitive, but always with herself, never with anyone else.

"Okay," he said.

"No, not 'okay.'" I did an impressive imitation of his deep voice. "Romantic love gets all the hype and it's bullshit. This love is more important and harder to live without. This is a love like family."

He raised his hands in surrender. "Let's drop it."

I sputtered. I couldn't process an Eric argument ending with "let's drop it." We'd carried on a euthanasia debate for a week. Argued the merits and detractions of teen social media accounts for two weeks. And spent a good month on opposite sides of the GMO controversy, picking up with new arguments each time we saw each other. Even the rest of the debate team would get tired of us. My point being, the vipers were ready to go round after round on romantic vs. platonic love, and now I was just supposed to drop it?

I deflated slightly, but my outrage crested again. "You brought it up!"

"And I'm sorry I did." He smiled slightly.

Ugh. It was one of those semifunny things he did where the whole class would guffaw because they worshipped him. Meanwhile, I'd actually be funny and get half a chuckle, maybe.

"Why are you so obsessed with getting Jessica back?" I said. "You knew her, what? Six weeks, maybe two months? You could meet an Instagram model with two hundred thousand followers tomorrow or date any of the girls who fawn over you in the halls. She's completely interchangeable with a thousand other girlfriends. But a best friend? Someone who gets you? Who becomes a part of you? Who sees all your ugliness and weirdness and loves you? Someone you can tell anything to. Who sticks with you through boring stories, a show tunes stage, and helps you cover up breakouts and breakdowns? Can you claim any of that about your precious Jessica? Can you say that about anyone?"

Silence blanketed the cabin and I felt victorious, but then I got a distinct squishy feeling. Like I'd parallel parked on the first try, only to get out of the car and step right in dog shit. But I couldn't put my finger on why. He'd insulted me so I'd insulted him back. That was how things went with us.

The quiet and Eric's clenched jaw only happened when one

of us hit below the belt. When things went too far, too personal, and someone was reeling, but what had I said? All the stuff about Jessica was true and, really, a compliment to him. He could get any girl between the football thing, his money, and his looks. Part of him wanting to find her had to be the shock of a girl rejecting him. He'd never admit it, but that was likely the real reason he'd wanted to go on the trip. Because he always broke up with whomever he was dating. No one ever left Eric.

And then I realized what I'd done. I should never have gone on that tirade about best friends, specifically about him not having one. Not to Eric. Literally anyone but Eric. But I'd gotten swept up in the moment and I'd somehow forgotten.

Eric's best friend was dead.

And my former friends were right: Kelsie Miller was an asshole.

CHAPTER NINE

The All-Too-Brief Story of Eric and Jason

Around the same time Brianna Hoffman sat next to me in kindergarten, Eric and Jason Gallagher had become friends. At least, I couldn't remember them ever not being friends. Eric was an only child and Jay was a semiforgotten middle child wedged between two sisters, so they became as close as brothers. It was rare to see one without the other, two peas in a pod. If there was a choice, they worked together on projects; if there was a pickup game, they played on the same team.

I liked Jay. Everyone did. He was funny but at the same time softer, quieter than Eric. He was blond with freckles on his nose. Essentially, he was the Bri to Eric's Kelsie—the more laid back, likable version. Jay played football, but he was small and didn't shine like Mulvaney Ortiz. No one did, really. Eric was a year older than just about everyone because his dads had delayed kindergarten a year to give him a size and intelligence edge. Which he'd had already because he was unfairly blessed. But Eric and Jay balanced each other out.

At the start of sixth grade (because middle school is fantastic), two eighth-grade kids got it into their heads to bully Jay. They'd knocked books out of his hands in the hall and called him queer. Because they were the kind of assholes who found being gay to be some kind of insult. I didn't know if Jay was gay or not because he never talked about it. And it never mattered to me.

He ignored them, but it escalated. Lunches dumped on him, mean crap written on his locker, and each time he told Eric not to worry about it, not to retaliate. But Eric was furious because Jay was his closest friend and, of course, his dads were gay. After seeing the fresh graffiti, he'd yelled down the hall: Anyone have a problem with gay people like my dads? You can come say it to me right now.

No one answered.

One day, probably thinking he was alone, the boys tried to jump Jay outside of school. They got one hit in before they found themselves on the wrong end of Eric's fists. It became the one and only blemish on Eric's record.

Because of the school's zero-tolerance bullying policy and despite him absolutely destroying the two older kids, the school offered to not suspend Eric if he apologized. They reasoned that he was only protecting his friend, which wasn't quite how it went down. I was there—Eric had totally lost it on them after Jay was already safe—but close enough.

The problem was, Eric refused to apologize. He said it would be the same as saying he was sorry to the garbage for taking out the trash. So he was suspended.

He became a legend after that. For the few days he was gone, all anyone could talk about was Eric Mulvaney Ortiz. Even I'd reluctantly been impressed by him sticking up for his friend and taking the punishment. But rumors spun out and the cult of Eric was born.

That winter dragged on forever, as winters did in our frozen tundra. And even the hint of spring brought everyone outside. Unfortunately, it brought Eric and Jay to Saratoga Lake.

The lake froze over every winter. It was so solid that people drove trucks onto it and ice fished. (Why was a mystery to me.) But the thing was, it also unfroze quickly. One day it was ice, the next it was back to liquid.

The story was everywhere for months, and they all said the same thing: The boys were playing out on the ice, running across it, and Jay fell through a thin spot. Despite Eric screaming for help and even jumping into the frigid water to try to rescue him, Jay drowned. The paramedics were on the scene in minutes, but they couldn't save him. Eric had hypothermia; Jay was dead.

It was all a terrible, random event. A nightmare tragedy.

The whole town went to the funeral and it was the worst. All I kept thinking about for weeks was the idea of Bri disappearing under the ice. I woke up screaming plenty of times thinking about going to a funeral for her. And she did too.

We'd text each other heart emojis in the middle of the night just to be sure we were both okay.

There were a bunch of think pieces written later about whether middle school kids should've been allowed to attend the wake and see such a small coffin. The school tried to help. They brought in professionals to teach us how to cope, which was equal parts useless and taken advantage of because some kids realized the group therapies could get them out of tests.

In short, it was god-awful. And Eric was never the same. When the grief counselors left, and people moved on, everyone stopped mentioning Jay. No one wanted to rub salt in Eric's wound.

And then there was me.

CHAPTER TEN

At a loss for what to do, I shook took my hair out of my messy bun. It was still damp from my shower when it hit my neck and I put my blue scrunchie on my wrist. Actually, it wasn't my scrunchie. It was Bri's, but we'd traded so long ago that it was hard to remember who'd originally had what. That's what happened with best friends.

Guilt nagged at me for losing sight of what had happened to Eric's. For being cruel, intentionally or not.

"That was a dickish thing to say. I . . . I'm an asshole," I said.

I figured it was best not to tread directly on Jason territory again, but I hoped Eric knew I wouldn't have purposely gone there.

He relaxed his shoulders a little. "It was dickish, but apology accepted."

I hadn't actually apologized, but I guess admitting I was a jerk was enough.

He glanced over and I searched his face. He seemed to have really forgiven me, which . . . I mean, I would've held the grudge a little longer (aka forever). But we did have a temporary bond—a secret mission—so he was probably letting things slide.

Or he was just a better person.

Unfortunately, I was never able to leave good enough alone. "Really?" I asked. "I mean, I didn't mean to talk about . . . It wasn't a shot at him. I wouldn't do that."

"I know. It's . . ." He drew a breath like he was collecting himself. "It's almost refreshing to have someone bring him up again. Even if you are an asshole."

The corner of his lips lifted a little, and my heart sped up. For the first time ever, I fell victim to an Eric smile. It was like the sun clearing the clouds and casting a warm glow on my face until I got ahold of myself.

"I wasn't trying to imply a best friend matters less," he said. "I just . . . I know what it's like to want to talk about someone but feel like you can't because no one's asked."

It all hit me at once. The times he wanted to talk about Jay but thought he couldn't. How lonely that must've felt. All anyone had wanted was to prevent him from hurting more, but it'd had the opposite effect.

His hand rested on the gearshift. Without thinking about it, I reached out and took his hand. When my palm met his, it felt like an electric spark went off between us. From the look in his eye, Eric had noticed it too. Immediately, I withdrew my arm. He looked out the window to the left. I looked out the window to the right. My heart beat too fast. I really needed to get a grip. I was desperate, but not this frigging desperate.

"Did, uh . . . did we just have a moment there? I'm touched, Mulvaney." I clasped my hands and batted my eyelashes, trying to clear whatever the hell had just happened out of the air.

He took a long sip of coffee. Yes, coffee sounded lovely. I pounded more of mine. The cup had sweat in the holder and a drop of water hit my bare legs. I wiped it off with my palm

The movement drew his attention to my legs. Then he quickly looked away.

"What's with the getup?" he asked.

"'Getup'?" I said.

He gestured to what I was wearing. I'd gone fashion with a loose, off-the-shoulder top and tighter shorts, sparkly polish on my toes, and golden sandals. It was something close to what Bri usually wore, because I'd read a psych article about how people loved mirrors and I'd decided to try it. Because I was such a loser.

But that wasn't something I was willing to admit aloud.

"Who even uses that term? What's with *your* 'getup'?" I said. I used air bunnies and gestured to him, happy to be back to our normal dynamic.

He had on a short-sleeved button-down and jeans, and the shirt made his biceps look even bigger. Like the sleeves could barely contain the "guns."

The "gun show" thing was from my dad. He had no muscles

to speak of, but he would flex and try to sell my mom paper napkin tickets when she was angry. The poses would get increasingly ridiculous and the buy-it-now prices lower until she finally broke her stone face and laughed. But Eric didn't have the sense of humor for that.

"I just thought I should look nice when I see her again," he said. His short wavy hair was gelled and everything.

"Well, same," I said.

"But you don't normally wear shorts," he said.

Which was true, but why would he notice? Then again it was probably a keep-your-enemies-closer type of thing.

"Do you keep a diary of my outfits? Wait . . . my getups?" I said.

He stared at me then made the radio louder. And yes, music and silence was exactly what the trip called for. I thought he listened to rock, but instead he kept it on Hits 1, a pop station and my personal favorite. I didn't know why people pretended to be too good for pop. Pop was short for "popular," meaning: songs people liked. We made it through a few tunes and down to the Thruway, the road that would take us toward New York City and eventually over to Jersey. One state closer to our goal.

A slower song came on, and instead of changing it, he turned it up.

"Big fan?" I asked.

He stared wistfully. "It brings back memories. The last time I heard this song was when I was in Jessica's car. We'd gone for a drive, chasing thunderstorms, and after this came on, she pulled over and we slow danced on the side of the road."

It was official: my frenemy was making things up. It sounded like a scene out of a Nicholas Sparks movie (my dad had gone through a romance phase). But one look at Eric's dreamy stare told me it was a real moment he was remembering.

I couldn't resist rolling my eyes. Actually, I rolled them so hard, they hurt. "That can't possibly have happened."

"It did." He smiled slowly, and it was a type of pure, unguarded joy I'd rarely seen on him. The kind that had disappeared years ago when everything happened with Jay, and he became more of a man statue and less of a kid. And it was . . . attractive. In a way. Maybe to other people.

"She's just . . . perfection," he said.

When I thought of all the hell he'd been through, I knew he deserved some goodness. But instead of being happy for him, something twisted inside me. I was distinctly not happy.

I didn't know what to say so I put both my thumbs up with a fake excited look on my face.

"What a pleasure you are," he said.

The song changed and suddenly I was the one haunted. Because I knew this song. More than that, it had interwoven with a memory, one I didn't like to think about. It was the other time I'd been incapable of being happy for someone. And I hadn't known it then, but it would be the last time I saw Bri.

CHAPTER ELEVEN

Before Things Fell Apart

JULY, ONE MONTH AGO

After some deliberation, Bri had chosen Hits 1, my choice, over Teagan's snoozy Coffee House suggestion for her party. It was still playing through the Sonos speakers even though the going-away party had wrapped up. Bri, Teagan, and I were the last ones at her dad's house. We were helping her clean up before a planned sleepover.

I'd tried to be happy all night. I really had. But the truth was, I was too upset that Bri was going to leave to feel any real joy. Even as her flight got closer and closer, I'd kept thinking that she'd come to her senses or her mother would say something and she'd realize she should stay. It was one more year until college and she was best off staying at Carver.

But Bri really was leaving. Tickets were purchased and her car was scheduled to be shipped out. And now she'd accepted gifts and hugs goodbye. After a couple of vodka crans, I couldn't fake it any longer. With everyone gone, I pulled her aside.

"You're making a big mistake, you know," I said.

I'd only said it because: I knew she was.

I remembered Elaine Taylor before she divorced Bri's dad. She was as pretty as she was cold. But more important, I remembered Bri waiting for her when she'd promised to show. I remembered Bri's hopeful eyes scanning the crowd looking for her mom at school assemblies or during her vocal performances. Instead, she'd find her dad sitting alone. I remembered wrapping my arm around her shoulders as we'd walk to my house after her mother didn't pick her up in elementary school. I remembered sitting on the curb outside of middle school, waiting for my parents to get us because we'd missed the buses waiting for her mom, who never came. And the tears Bri shed when Elaine decided right before freshman year that she'd take the promotion in Seattle and leave her for good. Of course, she'd promised Bri she'd come back for summers, and those never materialized either.

And now Bri was leaving me for her.

I stood on the patio under the twinkle lights with a couple of empty Solo cups in my hands. The lake shimmered in the distance and the air smelled like flavored vodka and sickly sweet bug spray. It was so hot, and without a single breeze it was like the air was pressing on me.

Bri stood by the sliding-glass door with her arms folded. Her blond hair was perfectly swept to the side, her white dress fitted to a tee. She was five-six and could pull off long dresses well. But her face was skewed, her expression stormy.

"I've already made this decision and everyone else is so supportive," Bri said. "Why can't you be?"

"Fine," I said, tossing the cups into the garbage. "They're obviously right. You're right. Everyone is right but me. Great choice to go chasing after a mother who doesn't want you."

She narrowed her eyes at me and stared for a second before she spoke. "I'm sorry I sat next to you in kindergarten."

With that, she turned and walked back into her house. The sliding door banged behind her, sending a jolt down my spine. Bri never slammed doors. I stood there stunned for a second as Teagan stared at me through the window, her mouth agape.

I felt an urge to explain myself, to apologize, but I stayed put. There was no need to apologize because nothing I'd said had been incorrect. Harsh maybe, but her mother would only let her down again and Bri would be stranded out there alone and then what?

Angry all over again at the whole situation, I grabbed my purse off the table and texted my dad to get me as I left Bri's backyard.

I made it to the edge of her driveway as I kept looking back at Bri's house, thinking she would come out and talk to me, but she never did. It was just me, alone, picking at the grass and swatting mosquitoes until my parents' Subaru pulled up.

CHAPTER TWELVE

I leaned my head against the ergonomic headrest of Eric's BMW as my body became leaden. Getting Bri back was going to be a lot harder than I'd figured. It hadn't sunk in at the time, but Bri had told me that she was sorry she ever met me.

It wasn't as cut-and-dried as it seemed, though. Bri and I had talked after her going-away party. In fact, she'd texted me the next morning. We'd both kind of pretended like nothing had happened and I'd chalked it up to us drinking too much. We continued to send each other the usual gifs and memes. Looking back, maybe it wasn't as much as usual, but I figured she was busy packing up her entire life.

And, yeah, maybe I could've phrased it better, but what I'd said was, in fact, true—she was chasing after a mother who time and time again hadn't wanted to be there for her. Who always had an excuse. But even if I'd hurt her, wasn't I owed the benefit of the doubt? After a dozen years, didn't she know that I'd never mean to hurt her? Wasn't I entitled to a sliver of a second chance when she'd given her mom a thousand of them?

It made no sense that one sentence could shatter a twelve-year friendship. And it left me thinking there was something or someone else I was missing, some reason for her to ghost me. Maybe a nasty rumor whispered by Teagan or she'd found a new best friend in Seattle who'd replaced me. Or a new girlfriend who was taking up all her time. Or another increasingly unlikely conspiracy theory.

"God, it's a beautiful day," Eric said, peering up through the windshield.

I shook off my thoughts and glanced up too. It was okay outside. Blue sky, puffy clouds, kind of normal for the last Thursday in August. But we'd been weird since the hand-spark thing; he was probably trying to restart a conversation.

"We're down to talking about the weather, huh?" I said.

He shrugged. "It's a good travel day. We'll make decent time."

We were an hour into the trip and somewhere around Hudson, New York. That left another 3.5 hours in the car. An eternity.

"It's a waste of a day if you ask me." I kicked off my sandals and sat cross-legged. "Why don't we at least open the windows?"

The BMW was climate controlled and driving me to distraction. Mom had said that my dad and I were born to live in the wild, completely ignoring the fact that we resided with a feral child. But, she had a point. We both went bananas when we were cooped up too long. We loved fresh air—walking, hiking, anything that got us out. And the end of the summer was already happening. The good days were numbered before the definition of "good" changed in the fall.

Eric's brow wrinkled and he stared over at me. "You want to open the windows?"

"Yes!"

He looked utterly perplexed. "But . . . won't your hair get messed up?"

"Does that matter?" I asked.

My hair refused to do anything but hang off my head like a curtain. My long black locks never looked bad but also resisted looking good, so we were at an impasse. I didn't try much, and I always kept a hair tie around. Bri had been the opposite. She'd spend an hour styling her hair, going pin straight one day, beach waves the next. And I'd learned a ton about hair care from Teagan, from coconut oil to relaxants to weaves and all the work she put into it. But mine was plain old straight.

Eric frowned. "We're on the highway, though."

"So?"

"So it would be really windy." He avoided eye contact.

I stared for a second before his comments clicked into place. "Wait. You're worried about your hair? Seriously?"

His brown hair was too short to even get knotted.

"I think at this point we can assume I'm serious," he said.

"It takes me a while to do my hair and it'll get poufy if we put the windows down. And if you repeat that to anyone, I swear to God I will hunt you down for sport, Miller."

"Yeah, yeah." I shifted my lips to the side, hopefully making some kind of contemplative face. "But so what if it's poufy? I mean, you'll still be gor-ge-ous."

He shot me an unamused look. "I want it to be perfect."

He said it seriously. Like his hair was going to be the deciding factor between happily ever after and Jessica calling the authorities.

"You really spend your time like this, huh?" I said. "On perfect?"

"We can't all be like you." He spoke in a low tone, but the music was switching and I heard him in the lull.

"What does that mean?"

"Nothing."

"It obviously means something or you wouldn't have said it. And we've got nothing but time here. Do go on." I'd probably be insulted again, but I was too curious to stop. And, really, it wasn't going to be any worse than what he'd said in middle school.

I mock rested my chin on my hands. He ignored me and we went back to silently cooking in the luxury biodome.

"I just . . . it's the pressure," he said.

Enough time went by for his voice to startle me and for me to have completely forgotten what we were talking about. "What pressure?" I asked.

He gave me a disappointed look, the corner of his mouth pulling down. "Not that you seem to feel it at all."

I mulled it over, but I had nothing. "The pressure to have good hair?"

"No. I mean in general, in everything. At Carver. On the field. At home. For the future. The pressure to win, to always get the highest A, to be perfect. It's exhausting, but it seems to slide right off you. For years I thought it was an act, but I don't think it is. What's the secret?"

I squinted at him. He had to be joking. Of course I felt the pressure to be "something." That weight was inexorably linked with the privilege of going to a school like Carver. Only 125 students a year were allowed to enroll, and of those, so many went on to win academic honors, scholarships, awards. But for me what was bigger than the Carver pressure was the fact that my dad had sacrificed his dream for me to stay in school in Upstate NY. He was going to go to LA, but he put it off after I got into Carver. He called it a once in a lifetime opportunity for me. So I had to do great things. It wasn't a question of whether but what. And even in a sea of smart, hypercompetitive kids, where the pressure routinely caused rashes and breakdowns, Eric was my only real competition. What secrets did he think I had? He was the one who made it look easy: homecoming king, debate team captain, quarterback, academic pain in my ass.

"Well, I start by never being close to perfect," I said. "That way there's no temptation to pursue it. And that seems to lower everyone's expectations accordingly."

My comment seemed to bum him out and we careened back into silence. Pinpricks of guilt hit me for being dismissive.

"I don't think anyone is perfect, Eric," I said. "Some people think my little sister's great and look how wrong that is."

He stared at the windshield. "Being my dads' only child doesn't help with the pressure. It's like . . . it's all on me, just me."

I uttered a sigh of longing. "I had nine blessed years of solitude."

Hanna was kind of a miracle baby and that fact hadn't gone to her head. Not. At. All. My parents adopted me in part because they'd tried for years to have a baby and got nothing but heartache. Then boom, nearly a decade after I came in from Korea, they had the red gremlin. As an apology, they got me Snuggles, my Scottish Fold death machine who happened to like Hanna better.

"You don't mean that," Eric said. "You love your sister."

I totally meant it. And yes, I loved Hanna.

I shook my head. "I'd lie in traffic for her. But have you ever hung out with an eight-year-old? They're treasure-hoarding dragons and the treasure is the shit they stole from you."

He breathed out a laugh. "I think I would've liked to have grown up with a little brother or sister. I volunteer at the elementary school and I like it."

Of course he did.

He drummed his fingers on the steering wheel. "Do you ever wonder if you have biological siblings?"

The question had been posed to me dozens of times in many iterations—did I wonder about my "real" family, did I know anything about my biological parents? And the answers were all complicated, so I gave him my stock reply.

"Nah," I said. "But I'm pretty sure I have an evil twin somewhere in Seoul."

He arched an eyebrow. "You're not the evil one?"

I faked offense with my hand over my heart. "Obviously not."

"Well, now I just feel bad for Seoul," he said.

I laughed. A real, no pretenses outburst. For the first time in our lives, Eric had made me laugh.

CHAPTER THIRTEEN

We'd made pleasant, meaningless conversation about our families until the end of New York. His parents were doing well. Couldn't agree on whether to add a four-season room to their mansion or buy a boat. The troubles of Dr. and Mr. Mulvaney Ortiz were endless.

In Non-loaded-ville, I told Eric about my dad getting short-listed for the Light Project. Whoever won would get their script turned into a pilot, or their movie made into a short, along with a generous prize and travel to LA with accommodations for a month to workshop their talent and meet industry people. It was everything my dad wanted and deserved.

"Even if he doesn't win, being on the short-list could lead to him getting an agent," I said. That was my dad's big elusive goal. He'd been trying for years to land one.

"That's really cool," Eric said. "I hope he gets it."

"Me too. Either way, he now has the validation to keep

going. He's gotten so many rejections. It's been so hard on him."

The knot of guilt hit my empty stomach as it always did when I thought of my dad struggling in his writer's loft (our attic) in frigging Saratoga. He would've made it already if he'd been in LA and able to hobnob with executives. Talent sometimes got through in Hollywood, but friends were better. Yet he'd stayed for me. He was the antithesis of Elaine Taylor. I wasn't sure why Bri couldn't see what real parents were willing to sacrifice.

"This is the last stop for a while. Do you need anything?" Eric asked.

We were coming up on the Ramapo rest stop. I kind of needed to use the bathroom, but I could tell by his tone that he wanted to keep going. And we were getting along well enough, so I decided to be agreeable.

"I do, but let's get to Jersey. I can wait for the next one." I drained the last of my mega iced coffee.

"Okay."

Then, because my luck was the worst, we hit a sea of red brake lights a few miles into New Jersey. Route 17 was a connector between the Thruway and the Jersey Turnpike. It was full of rich-people stores and dealerships, and seemingly every resident of the state needed to be there that very minute.

I shook my foot, regretting another of my choices that summer, because immediately I had to use the bathroom.

We crawled along the three-lane road. By the time we reached the end of the interminable four-mile strip, I really needed to pee. I was starting to eye gas stations. Was I willing to risk the certain bathroom horrors contained under lock and key?

"The Turnpike is coming up and there are rest stops every few miles," Eric said, glancing down at my flapping foot. "We'll stop at the first one."

"Okay, cool."

Eric continued talking, but it was hard to focus because MY GOD, I HAD TO PEE. All I could think about was what I'd give for a toilet and why I failed at preparing for things ahead of time. Little things like maybe not drinking enormous iced coffees on road trips. Or slightly bigger things like friends breaking up with me and leaving me to survive senior year alone, or my having to make choices about my entire future at only seventeen years old.

As we got onto the Turnpike, I felt fairly certain we'd never find a bathroom again. I'd have to figure out how to pee in shorts in a Dunkin' cup and/or Eric would fling me out of his car.

Finally, the signs appeared for a rest stop. My salvation. My dream.

Everything moved too slowly, even though Eric was speeding. He'd taken it off cruise and was driving in the left, passing cars. Maybe he was being considerate or maybe he had to go too.

We finally pulled into the parking lot. I wasn't a doctor or pre-pre-med like Eric, but I was pretty certain a bladder could explode. Mine might be the first documented case.

Eric shut off the engine. "Want to take a stroll and stretch or—"

Note: it was NOT the moment for Eric to be funny for the second time in his life.

"Shut up, shut up, shut up," I chanted.

I half ran/half waddled out of the car, slamming the door and praying there wouldn't be a line. Please, dear ladies'-room gods: no unloading tour buses.

I was so fixated on getting to the bathroom that I stopped paying attention to the busy parking lot.

It happened in an instant: A white Mercedes speeding down the lane, someone yelling out "Kelsie." I turned my head and froze like a deer in oncoming Benz headlights only to be suddenly yanked up into the air and pulled backward. My sandal went flying as my legs left the ground, but somehow the car missed me. Strong arms surrounded me as I spun around. I faced Eric, who was holding me.

What the hell had just happened?

We stood there, breathing heavily. We were almost chest to chest, but I wasn't tall so more like my chest to his stomach. His eyes locked with mine and the spark went off again. The same one from when our hands touched.

The moment broke a second later when someone punched the back of a car. In true Jersey style, some random guy was shouting at the driver to "slow the f*** down, you f***face, you almost killed that f***ing girl."

It finally clicked. I was almost mowed down by a car. And the driver had been kind enough to brake to see if I was roadkill. The fact was, I was only alive because Eric had grabbed me, picked me up, and pulled me back.

Eric, my nemesis, had saved me.

My brain frizzed and shorted out.

"Jesus." Eric dropped one of his arms and ran his hand over his hair. His fingers shook, but his other arm held me tight. "Are you okay?"

On the plus side, I'd temporarily forgotten about my epic need to pee and hadn't soiled myself, so aces. I was doing very well.

"Yeah, yes," I said.

I went to take a step and realized my shoe was missing. So . . . perhaps not quite that well.

Eric looked both ways (what a concept) and then ran, grabbed it off the ground, and came back to me. He knelt on the pavement and held my sandal. I didn't need him to kneel, but as I tried to get my shoe on, I wobbled. So maybe I did. He wrapped his hand around my calf, steadying me, and I put my hands on his broad shoulders, now trembling from the near-miss, but somehow I got my toes in.

Without a word, Eric stood, took my hand, and walked us into the building. It wasn't until we were at the entrance of the restrooms that he let go.

I lucked out—no line in the bathroom. I raced into one of the stalls and somehow did not pee my shorts. Go me!

I would've focused on the amazingness of modern indoor plumbing, except my brain had come back online and I was consumed by what had happened with Eric. How he'd managed to get to me and toss me out of harm's way, that he'd called me Kelsie, how shaken he'd been, the sweetness of him finding my sandal and kneeling so I could get my foot in. The way he held my hand and made sure I was safe all the way into the building.

And, okay, yeah, that spark. Twice.

After an eternity peeing, I washed my hands and stared in the mirror. My eye makeup had held up remarkably well. I adjusted my shirt, dabbed on lip gloss, and ran my fingers through my hair but stopped. What the hell was I trying to do? Impress him? First of all, we'd just been in the car together for two hours. Second, we'd known each other since we were five. And last and most important, we were on this trip to win back his ghost girl-friend.

His can't-live-without-you, slow-dance-in-the-rain, Ivy-League Instagram model.

I sighed. Even if he weren't dating some kind of dream girl, I already knew he thought I was repulsive. He'd said it himself years ago.

I hit myself on the side of my head trying to chase out my thoughts. He didn't like me, definitely not like that. All Eric had done was not let me die in front of him. Which was still some-thing, but not what I was imagining. Not to mention: I didn't like him, either. He was an ass-kissing, annoyingly popular, rich perfectionist standing in my way of academic solo glory.

Disgusted with my delusions, I threw my gloss back into my bag. I looked fine, but inside Kelsie Miller was a hot mess. Once upon a time I had two friends to help me pull myself back together, but now I was on my own.

CHAPTER FOURTEEN

Before Everything Went Wrong

AUGUST OF LAST YEAR

"You sure you'll be okay?" Mom asked, pulling up to Fasig-Tipton.

Fasig-Tipton was a Saratoga auction house open just four nights a year—that was all they needed to sell millions and millions of dollars of thoroughbred horses. What had started off as a racing industry thing had become a uniquely Saratoga social event—a place to "be seen."

I didn't have much (any) interest, but Bri did. Her dad had stakes in a few horses and his racing group got special access, so she'd invited me and Teagan to join them that Monday night.

"Yes, I'll be fine," I said.

Mom side-eyed the fairly low-cut dress I'd bought at Bri's insistence. "All right. Call me if you need anything—no questions asked."

"Love you," I said.

Mom gave my white dress another skeptical once-over before smiling. "Have fun. But be safe."

I could not handle another safety lecture. I nearly hopped out of the moving car, but I managed to wait for her to put it in park.

"We're going to be with Bri's dad," I said. "I'll be fine. Thanks for the ride."

I got out of the Subaru and was barely six feet away before I realized why she'd side-eyed my outfit. I was one of maybe four Asian people in town so I was used to stares, but this was something different. This was a lot of old pervy guys leering at me.

Gross.

Ignoring them, I went inside the pavilion to find Bri. I looked around from the auctioneer to the crowd and spotted Teagan easily. She liked to say she and I were the ink spots in the milk, as there were just about as many Black people as Asian in the town. For better or worse, we stood out.

But that night it came in handy as I made my way to their row. Bri's dad was all smiles when he saw me. He gave me a hug then turned me toward his racing partners.

"This is Bri's brilliant best friend, Kelsie," he said. "They go to Carver together, and Kelsie is at the top of their class. This girl is going to change the world."

Heat warmed my face. It was written in stone somewhere that parents had to be embarrassing. Even when they weren't yours. But Bri's dad had known me for so long, he was like an unofficial uncle.

The guys had stood up out of politeness and said some version of "nice to meet you." I waved before sitting with Bri and Teagan.

"Elderly sausage fest up in here," Teagan whispered, leaning over Bri to talk to me.

I tried not to laugh but snorted/coughed instead, and one of the guys, Chuck something, smiled at me. He was a little younger than Bri's dad, but not by much.

"I can't take you two anywhere," Bri said with a laugh. She smacked both of us with her program.

"You love us," I said.

"I do." Bri gripped my hand, then focused on the next horse they brought in.

The auctioneer spoke at an unbelievably fast pace and had his different helpers in tuxedos raise the bid until the horse sold for $400,000.

Yeah, people spent the equivalent of college and med school tuition on a year-old horse.

It was how the other half lived. Or . . . well, the one percent.

Bri was into it, though. Her dad had taught her what to look for, and she'd made all kinds of notes on her program.

"I'm bored," Teagan said after we'd sat through about ten more sales.

"You're not alone," I stage-whispered.

Bri rolled her eyes at both of us but smiled. "Let's go out to the paddocks."

We left the pavilion and made our way outside, where they

trotted the horses around. The fancy paddock area had tables where people were eating dinner for some reason, bars to rest drinks, and packed crowds watching the horses or just people watching.

The three of us found a good viewing spot, and it was oddly interesting to watch the young horses parade by.

"All right, I need to go find the bathroom," Teagan said.

"Ugh, me too," Bri said. "How about you, Kel?"

"I'm good. I'll save our spots," I said. We'd wormed our way into a position with a bar to put our stuff down. I didn't want to give it up.

"Cool, back soon," Bri said.

After they left, I looked at the book Bri had marked up. I'd never understood the program for the horses. It was all about bloodlines—the horse's parents and what the horse's relatives had earned in races. It was as ridiculous as it sounds.

"See anything you like?" a voice asked.

I turned and Chuck had come up behind me with two drinks in his hands. He rested them on the bar in front of us.

He pushed one toward me. "For you."

"Really?" I asked. Like most teens in town, I was always trying to score alcohol—but that was mainly for my friends. I didn't drink much.

"Cheers." He lifted his glass and I lifted mine, then took a sip.

"I guessed at rum and Coke, but if anyone asks, it's just Coke." Chuck winked at me. He had eyes bluer than his suit jacket.

"Thanks," I said. "What are you drinking?"

"Scotch," he said. "Eighteen year. So . . . your age?"

"Two years older than me, actually," I said.

"Christ," he said with a laugh. "You're too stunning to be so young."

I didn't know what to say to that. It was the kind of compliment I rarely, if ever, got. Normally I'd hear how intelligent I was, not pretty. He was handsome enough in a dad kind of way, but he had to be twice my age.

"How old are you?" I asked.

He smiled and shook his head. "Let's talk about better things."

I finished the rum and Coke and Chuck flagged down a waiter. There wasn't cocktail service, but money bought a lot of things in town.

"I used to come up to Saratoga with my parents when I was a kid," Chuck said, moving closer. "I always wanted to own a racehorse, and now I do."

The waiter came back and dropped off two drinks the color of iced tea.

"What's this?" I asked.

"Long Island Iced Tea," Chuck said. "Try it. It's good. They gave me two by accident so . . . all yours."

It was actually pretty good. Later I'd find out it was made from four liquors and very strong. I'd also come to doubt that they'd given him two by mistake. But that night I hadn't noticed as we watched the horses. Chuck talked to me about commercial real estate, which I had zero interest in, but he was entertaining enough. Bri and Teagan were nowhere to be found the whole time, which wasn't surprising. There'd probably been a bathroom line or they ran into people. Because of her parents' bakery, Teagan knew just about all of Saratoga.

I was on the second iced tea when Chuck moved my hair off my shoulder and got so close, his pants brushed against my dress.

"It's prettier over to the side," he said.

"Um, okay," I said.

I didn't like a stranger touching me, but he was nice to get me the drinks and he was pleasant enough. The night was getting fuzzy around the edges, and it was hard to care much about anything. Which was nice since at Carver I had to care about everything all the time.

"David says you're a good girl," Chuck said. "Is he telling the truth?"

David was Bri's dad.

"Does he lie to you a lot?" I asked.

Chuck laughed and put his hand against the bar, kind of boxing me in. I backed up to put a little space between us.

"Isn't it tiring being so good all the time?" Chuck leaned in, closing the gap, and whispered in my ear. "Maybe you should try being bad."

I didn't know what he meant, but my brain was working

slowly. It was one of the reasons I didn't like drinking. This all felt wrong, but my mind was mud and I couldn't articulate why.

"Um, hey," Bri said.

I jumped away. The part of my brain that knew it wasn't right for us to be so close screamed: he's twice your age and trying to get you drunk! The looks on Bri's and Teagan's faces told me I was right: something was very off with all of this.

Chuck wasn't fazed though. He stood straighter and smiled. "I was just keeping your friend company."

"I can see that," Bri said.

"Well, we're back now, so . . ." Teagan made a shooing motion with her hand. I'd never seen anyone look so annoyed in a crop top.

"It's fine," I slurred.

"What are you drinking?" Bri scanned the bar and frowned.

"Tea," I said. For some reason I found it hilarious. I laughed and I was the only one.

"She seems a little tipsy and should probably go," Chuck said. "I can give her a lift home."

"We'll take care of her," Bri said.

"You didn't seem to care how long she was alone here," he said.

Bri swung around and stared at him. She was a few inches shorter than he was, but you'd never know it from the way she stepped up to him.

"You should probably go find my dad before I do," she said.

They stared at each other for a second before Chuck adjusted his jacket. "Of course. Nice to meet you, Kelsie. Ladies."

"Bye, Chuck," I giggled.

Bri and Teagan exchanged a look.

"Okay, it's time for a walk," Teagan said.

"Really?" I asked.

"Oh, yeah," Bri said.

They escorted me out, each taking an arm as I wobbled. I barely made it a block from Fasig-Tipton before I threw up. The first time.

Bri held my hair out of the way and Teagan called her brother, Mack, to get us and bring us to Bri's house. I can't remember much of the ride except for Bri taking my phone and texting my mom pretending to be me to get permission to sleep at her house. Mostly I remembered the breeze on my face from the open window. Mack was very concerned I'd puke in his Nissan and kept telling me he'd pull over if I just said the word, but somehow I made it to Bri's house, specifically her toilet.

"I love you guys," I said from the floor of her bathroom.

Bri and Teagan were sitting by her jetted tub with crackers and water on a towel in a little floor picnic.

"We love you too," Bri said. "No more Long Island Iced Teas. Ever."

"Or creepshow old dudes," Teagan said.

"He was nice," I slurred.

Teagan shook her head. "He was a sleeze, but we've got you."

Bri wrapped her arms around me and I leaned my head on hers. Unfortunately, shifting around made the horizon tilt.

"I . . . I think I'm going to puke again," I said.

They rushed into action, Teagan taking my hair as Bri rubbed my back.

The next morning we all woke up on the blanket and pillow nest they'd made on the bathroom floor like nothing had happened. But I knew they'd gotten me out of a mess in more ways than one.

CHAPTER FIFTEEN

I came out of the rest stop bathroom to find Eric waiting for me. He leaned against a wall, facing the ladies' room, but he was staring at his phone. My stomach flipped when I saw him, my steps shaky, but it must've been the aftereffects from the whole almost-roadkill thing.

Eric looked up from his phone, and something had changed. The expression on his face was a world away from when we went to the restrooms. He was . . . cold now.

Maybe the near death had affected him, too.

"Hey." I walked up to him and softly punched his shoulder.

He glanced at my hand like I was annoying him. Even though I'd just recalibrated myself in the bathroom mirror, I was still thrown off by the one-eighty. He'd held me in the parking lot and took my hand through the people milling around inside the rest stop and waited until I disappeared into the bathroom. That Eric was totally different from the one standing in front of me now.

I didn't know what to do with my hand, so I shoved my fingertips into the uselessly small pocket of my shorts.

"I just wanted to say . . . thanks. For before," I said.

He shrugged. "Oh. Yeah. It's nothing."

"Yeah, totally," I mumbled.

It was frigging awkward. Weirder than weird. Worse than when we'd started the road trip. As we idled there, my soul wanted to astral project out of my body to escape that level of discomfort.

Right on cue, my stomach gurgled in the most caveman-like way.

He raised an eyebrow. "Hungry?"

Great, so we were back to jabbing at each other. I was glad I hadn't bothered with any more makeup. I would've come out as Desperate the Clown.

But I was, in fact, hungry, and maybe food would take the edge off things. In the chaos of my dad's good news and trying to get out of my house, I'd had only a bite of English muffin before Eric had pulled into my driveway at nine on the dot.

Right as I was thinking about lunch, my stomach roared again. It sounded like a walrus bellow, and even Eric's composure cracked with a laugh.

"Yes. It appears I need a triple bacon burger, stat," I said.

He knit his eyebrows at me. "A triple?"

We walked over to the Wendy's.

"Yes. I take it Jessica never ate triple bacon burgers," I said.

"Well . . . she was vegan and cruelty-free," he said.

I raised my eyebrows. "Man . . . she sounds like a blast."

"She was. There's nothing wrong with being vegan or cruelty-free," he said. "Those are good things—great things, actually. But, she did freak one time because I told her Caesar dressing has eggs and usually anchovies in it. Threw her salad to the ground and stomped her feet. Croutons went flying everywhere and she yelled at the waiter." He smiled and then his smile faded. "I mean, it was totally understandable that she was upset. If you don't eat animal products and then you do, you can get sick."

"Uh-huh," I said. We could pretend flinging salad was normal, tempered behavior.

We waited in the short line. I got a triple bacon cheeseburger, and Eric, after a ridiculous amount of deliberation, got the same. We split fries—well, he paid for a large and said I could have some. I was all good on beverages, but I grabbed water for the road.

We took our trays of seriously overpriced food and picked a booth. I suspected Eric didn't allow anyone to eat in his Beamer, so I hadn't even suggested it.

I dove into my burger as soon as my ass hit the seat. But Eric looked distracted. He hadn't even unwrapped his when I was already through two huge bites.

I finished chewing and swallowed. "What?"

"Huh?" He had the same disoriented look as Bri when she came back from being lost in her own brain.

"You've been off since I got out of the bathroom," I said.

"I . . . it's nothing," he said.

I decided to roll with that lie, but then he pulled his phone out and opened Instagram. I was amazed he'd gone our whole trip without looking, except that he had blockers on his phone while driving. I stole some of his fries while he watched a video. He was as intently focused on his screen as he was on the AP Physics exam.

Triple bacon was heaven, and he was bringing me down with his furrowed brow and pained stares.

"What. Is. Wrong?" I said.

He sighed and put his phone down. "It's probably nothing."

"We can go another round of yeah everything is great or you can actually talk to me, if you want," I said. "Up to you."

"It's her Instagram Reel." Eric turned his phone toward me.

I watched a startlingly hot girl (Jessica) pose in a variety of places. Then the video panned over to other good-looking, although not as good-looking, friends. End scene.

"What's the issue?" I asked.

"Like I said, it's probably nothing, but there was a guy," he said.

There was. Right at the end. He'd been taking the video and panned to himself. He was South Asian, and nearly as handsome as Jessica was pretty, and that was saying something.

"Do you think he's her new boyfriend?" I asked.

"No!" Eric said it so forcefully, he startled me, and I accidentally dropped my pilfered fry. He unwrapped his burger but didn't start eating.

"He's someone she knows from Philly. He's a sophomore at UPenn and into photography, so he helps her with her social media, which makes him, like, a work friend. But she has a rule against having guys in her Insta. She thinks it ruins her brand. I'm just surprised to see him on there—maybe she forgot to crop him out."

I put two and two together. "You were never on her Insta."

He shook his head. "She was on mine, but she didn't want me to tag her. I understood. She has a certain image to portray. He was just doing a shoot and they must've forgotten to cut the last part."

Yeah, there was no way he was just a work friend doing a shoot, but okay.

I put my burger down. "Eric . . ."

He stared at me—a warning shot. He wasn't going to be open to even the idea that she'd moved on, despite the fact that it was most likely what had happened. And I had . . . well, I had zero relationship experience to draw from. There was my crush on Ryan Culligan, and I'd unfriended him after he posted a pic with his arm around a girl because I'd gotten jealous. Which was silly because he and I had never been anything, but explain that to my fourteen-year-old heart.

Then I had an idea.

"Have you tried jealousy?" I asked.

Eric stared at me.

"Have you tried posting anything to make Jessica jealous? To make her notice you? I mean, I've tried to post on socials to get Bri to remember what she was missing—our town, our fun, our routine. Can't say it's worked, but it could be worth a try."

He sat back and folded his arms. "That may work. . . . What are you thinking?"

As usual I just went where my brain took me: I was a girl and we were eating lunch together. This could've been a romantic road trip. If we were totally different people.

"Here, let's take a couple of selfies," I said. "Funny faces, then silly, biting into burgers poses, then looking at each other. You can post them to your stories."

"You'd . . . help me?" He seemed downright skeptical.

"Hey, what are desperation buddies for?"

He laughed.

"I know I'm not as good looking as she is, but I am female and that should do," I said.

He opened his mouth to argue, but I put my hand up. I didn't want to do one of those fake "no, really, you're pretty" things with him. I wasn't ugly, but I wasn't her, either.

I pushed my meal over to his side, like we were those weirdos who sat next to each other in booths. He held out his phone and put the camera in selfie mode. I revived the roll of duck face for another pic, then we did one as carnivores biting into our huge burgers. Both turned out perfectly.

"This last one should ooze sexual tension," I said, lowering my voice as far as it would go.

"Done," he said.

He ran a hand over his hair then faced me instead of the phone, and it was . . . different. He looked at me like there was nothing else in the world. Not Bri. Not Jessica. Not the incredibly bad music in the rest stop. Just us. Then he snapped the picture.

We both looked at it. He was a great actor. It looked like we were ready to go at it in the plastic booth.

"It's perfect." I cleared my throat and rapidly sat back across from him. Because for a split second he'd even fooled me.

"You . . . you really think this'll work?" His finger hovered over his phone screen.

Did I? Well, if she'd moved on with the hot camera guy, then no. But jealousy was a strange animal. I didn't know if Jessica was the jealous type, but something about the number of selfies and hashtags she used struck me as insecure. And jealousy was insecurity, right? That was my feeling as I'd seen a girl with Ryan, thought about Teagan's new role in Bri's life, even as I envied teens who'd figured out the next twenty years of their futures. It was all based on things I was anxious about.

I shrugged. "Worth a shot."

He nodded and posted the Story.

CHAPTER SIXTEEN

Eric couldn't stop checking his Stories to see if Jessica had watched.

(She hadn't.)

But people from school were watching in droves and . . . yeah, we hadn't exactly thought that part through. We'd need to do damage control later.

Once we were back in his car and buckled in, Eric's phone dinged and he grabbed at it. His face fell as he looked at the screen, then he activated the Do Not Disturb and tossed his phone into the cup holder.

"Everything . . . okay?" I asked.

"Yes." He started the car.

"Mm-hmm, you seem really good," I said.

He side-eyed me as we drove out of the parking lot and pulled up to the line at the nearby gas station. For some reason, New Jersey didn't allow people to pump their own gas, so we waited our turn for an attendant. Eric still had half a tank, but he wasn't the kind of person to let his car get much below that. My dad, on the other hand, had set personal bests for how long he could ride around on E.

I took my phone out of my bag and checked it. No new messages aside from nosy classmates who'd seen Eric's Insta Story and my mom reminding me to be safe. I threw my phone back into my purse and slouched in my seat, trying not to blush.

"Are you okay?" he said.

"If you won't answer, I won't answer."

"It . . ." He pursed his lips. "It wasn't Jessica."

"I could tell," I said.

I figured it was people from school blowing up his phone too, but he seemed really troubled.

The silence stretched out and the gas line was going nowhere even though the BMW had the fancy Euro right-side tank, which should've put us in the faster lane. As I sat with my car envy, I realized I needed to get over Eric's good fortune. Being jealous wouldn't give me more money or him less. And he wasn't smug about it like other people in our class.

"It was just my mom messaging, by the way," I said. "She's got jokes today."

"I love your mom," he said.

Although I loved her more than the moon and stars, that wasn't a high schooler thought to share. So I sat on it.

"She's all right," I replied.

"No, she's really great." He got that distant, faraway gaze again.

"Eric, look, we're on a trip that didn't happen. You can tell me things. You can be honest and drop the façade. It's exhausting just to watch it. What happens on this stalker road trip, stays on this stalker road trip. I swear."

I put up two fingers like I was taking an oath. He cracked a smile.

"It's . . ." He took a deep breath. "It's my surrogate."

Okay, not what I'd thought he was going to say.

"Your surrogate . . . mother?" I asked.

"She . . . yeah. The woman who gave birth to me was also the egg donor, so technically she's my biological mother, but I don't know what to call her."

He trailed off and stared at the steering wheel and I wondered if he was second-guessing telling me something so personal. In school I would've just let it go, but for some reason I wanted him to confide in me.

"Okay . . . she texted you?" I asked.

"Yeah. Since I turned eighteen, she's been trying to contact me."

He sighed heavily.

"Why eighteen?" I had many questions, but that was the first one out.

"Something to do with the contract she had with my dads. I don't think she was supposed to contact me ever, but legally she could once I became an adult. You haven't had that happen?"

I shook my head. "No. It's different for me, though."

"How?" he asked.

It was a little strange talking to him so openly about this stuff, but on the other hand it felt natural. Eric was one of three people I knew who had a complicated origin story. I was adopted as a baby, Julia who was a year younger than us was adopted through the foster care system, and Eric was born via surrogacy. Because his dads had found a surrogate who was similar in background to Mr. Mulvaney, most people didn't know who he was genetically tied to. That had been done by design, so all of them would appear related.

For me, no one ever thought I was biologically related to either of my parents.

"Adoption from another country kind of severs all ties," I said. "I don't think my biological mother would be able to find me even if she tried really hard."

Eric stared ahead thoughtfully. "Have you ever wanted to look for her?" he asked. Then he frowned. "Never mind. You don't have to answer that. It's personal."

It was, but we were right in the center of super-sensitive issues and I didn't mind talking about it. My parents had always been open and honest about my adoption, and they'd also wanted to know how I felt about it through the years. It was never a taboo thing. To me it was as natural as how biological children talk about the night they were born.

"It's okay," I said. "No, I haven't." Then I realized it sounded like I hadn't given any thought to finding my birth mother. "I mean, maybe that's wrong, I don't know. But my mom is my mom. I appreciate my biological mother, but I don't think I'd ever look for her. And I'm okay with us not being able to find each other."

He nodded along. "I feel the same."

A warm current flowed through me from Eric not only understanding where I was coming from but feeling the same way.

"I just wish she wasn't trying to contact me," he said. "My dads are my dads. They're my family. To me, she's just the woman who gave them a donor egg. But she can't seem to leave it at that. She even moved to Albany from Virginia recently. And . . . I have a brother."

"What?" I shouted.

Eric pulled up to the gas pump and calmly asked the attendant to fill it with premium gas, like he hadn't just dropped a bombshell on me. Then he put the window back up.

"Well, a half brother. He's twelve. My . . ."—he paused—"my surrogate got married and had another baby years after me. And now not only does she want to meet me—she said they've watched all my football games, online or in person—but she wants me to meet him, too. At some point—apparently it's up to me."

Wow. That was . . . a lot. A lot, a lot.

"What do your dads say about all this?" I asked. I didn't know Mr. Mulvaney as well as I knew Dr. Ortiz, but they were both good people. Because of that, I bet they'd been no help.

Eric frowned. "They want me to do what I think is best."

Winner, winner—zero help.

"I'm sure they're not telling me how they really feel, because they want it to be my choice," he said. "But they put the no-contact thing into the contract because they didn't want there to be us and then this other family out there somewhere, but now there is, and I . . . I can't unknow it. I have to make a decision and not only is it for me, but I'm deciding for a kid I had no clue existed up until a few weeks ago."

I nodded, but I couldn't fully wrap my head around it. My birth mother finding me was never something I wished for or thought much about because of the zero probability. My dad had a better chance at winning an Oscar (and yes, I'd caught him more than once doing an acceptance speech in the mirror). But how would that have felt? To not only have her trying to contact me but also to share that I had a sibling? To be linked by genes but not know them at all? I would've felt sideswiped at the very least. Blown apart would be more accurate.

"I . . . don't know what to say," I said.

"It's all right," Eric said. "I just . . . I wish she'd never contacted me."

We sat in silence for a second as the gas pump clicked to a stop. I was glad he felt comfortable talking to me, even though he seemed done with the subject. But I was still trying to process what it would feel like if my biological mother found me after all this time.

"What is it with women getting back in touch lately?" I asked.

Eric paid and we got back onto the Turnpike.

"Who else got back in touch?" he asked.

"Well, the whole reason Bri moved to Seattle was because her crappy, absentee mom finally asked her to go live with her."

I folded my arms and couldn't resist stewing over the unfairness of it all. I remembered when she'd first made the offer, and Brianna had been stunned. Her eyes had taken on that spacey, dazed look as she told me about it. I'd said: "You're going to say no, right? Who leaves Carver? Who leaves any school to transfer right before their senior year?" And Brianna had shaken off her stupor and said: "Yeah, yeah, you're right."

But, of course, she'd changed her mind.

"Elaine wasn't really an absentee mom," Eric said. "I remember her. I always thought it was cool that she let us call her Elaine."

I shook my head like I hadn't heard him correctly. "Are you serious? She was awful. She'd stand Bri up all the time."

"She was flaky, but she had to have shown up some of the time; otherwise, I wouldn't have known her at all," he said.

Okay, yes, she'd try to make up for the regular failures by doing extraordinary and occasional things like treating the class to a mobile petting zoo visit or bringing in a former pop star to sing a song with Bri during her talent show performance. Huge, splashy things that everyone remembered, because she'd forget to pick up her own daughter the following Thursday.

"Didn't they go to Italy together not too long ago?" Eric asked.

"Sophomore year," I said.

Her mother had taken Bri to the Amalfi Coast for her birthday, and it seemed like they hit every spa over there as Bri had posted a photo dump of their luxury adventure. Money, Elaine Taylor had. She was CFO of some tech company.

"And didn't Bri go with her to China?" Eric added.

"Taiwan. Once. Her mom had a work thing out there and flew her out," I said. "Bri was alone most of the time."

She was until her mother finished the event and then they went to Macau and "stopped in" Hawaii for more spas and beaches on their way back. Bri heavily remembered the second half and conveniently forgot the first half, where she was all alone and bored.

"Bri went skiing in Aspen most winters," Eric said. "Wasn't that with her mother?"

I cursed the super-small nature of Carver. Bri and Eric were friendly, but not exactly friends, yet everyone knew everyone's business so well. I didn't know why people even bothered posting things on social media when all the updates were floating through the halls constantly.

"Those were vacations," I said. "Some of them were work trips, and I don't see how they count."

Eric shrugged. "I'm just saying she doesn't sound like an absentee parent."

I stared at him. "She literally left her."

Eric shook his head. "You think she's horrible because you're comparing Elaine to your mom and dad. But most parents aren't as good as yours. Most families aren't. What Bri had wasn't perfect, but it was hers, you know?"

I opened my mouth, then closed it. I . . . didn't know. Deep down I couldn't understand her trying with her mom or constantly forgiving her. I couldn't understand her making a decision that was the polar opposite of what I would've chosen. But maybe my point of view had come from having a family like mine. In my head, Bri and I were like sisters, but that wasn't reality. Bri would say my house was like a sitcom family and claim she was lucky to have landed the role as recurring guest star. I'd asked her what she meant by that, and she said that we always laughed and joked, but at the end of the day we loved each other to pieces. She said not every family was like mine. I hadn't realized she was talking about her own family.

I closed my eyes.

I'd never tried to see where she was coming from because I thought I knew. But maybe there had been distance between us long before she'd ever moved to Seattle.

CHAPTER SEVENTEEN

Kelsie's Log of Failure

DAY THIRTY-FIVE OF NO CONTACT

Kelsie Miller's Phone
Bri Bri Hoffman

I think . . . I think I finally get it.

I shouldn't have been so judgmental about you
choosing to be with your mom, and I wish I
hadn't said those things at your party. I was just
too worried she'd let you down and you'd be
alone out there. But I wasn't happy for you the
way I should've been. I didn't know how to be

CHAPTER EIGHTEEN

We continued on through New Jersey, hurtling toward Philadelphia, a city I knew almost nothing about aside from cheesesteaks and the seventies movie *Rocky*.

There were roughly thirty miles left on our trip, and we were no closer to having a plan to find our exes than when we'd left.

I glanced at the speedometer and the needle hovered between eighty and ninety miles per hour. Time and traffic were blurring by.

"Going a little fast there?" I said.

"Sorry." Eric eased off the gas, and we fell back under eighty.

"Nervous?" I asked.

As soon as we'd started seeing signs for Philadelphia, my heart had taken up residence in my throat. What if we couldn't find Bri? We would've gone all this way for nothing. And what if we did find her and she hated me and ended all hope of us being friends again? That would be even worse than the monthlong limbo. Although not talking to her had sucked, how could I live without at least the chance of patching things up?

I'd messaged her thinking I'd cracked the code of why she'd stopped talking to me, but as had become usual, she hadn't responded. Maybe there was no mystery to solve. Maybe it was just over. And nothing in life, no movies with my dad, no books I'd read, no classes I'd aced, had prepared me for dealing with a best friendship ending.

"No, I'm not nervous. Just anxious to get there," Eric said.

It was a silly question. I couldn't recall a time where I'd seen Eric nervous. Not during speeches, or on the field, or even when debating. He was impossible to rattle. Which was why his shaken expression in the parking lot had been so surprising.

"I guess no matter what happens, at least you saw the campus," he said.

I stared at him.

"It's on your list because it's one of the Ivies, right?" he asked.

I chewed my lip. "Oh . . . yeah."

We sat in the quiet of that lie. I looked over to see if I'd fooled Eric. I hadn't. Not for a second.

"What was it you said before?" he asked. "Ah, yes, what happens on the stalker trip stays here. You can tell me what's actually up."

Could I? Through secrets and near-death experiences, we'd built a unique bridge of trust, but Eric was still Eric.

I shook my head. "You wouldn't understand."

"Try me."

"It's . . ." I sighed.

The whole thing had been on my mind for months, and even though he probably wouldn't understand, sometimes just saying thoughts aloud helped. My dad called it: talking things out. He'd do that when he was stuck on a plot point.

"I said that thing about the Ivies because it's what people expect to hear," I said. "To be honest, I don't know where I want to go because I don't know what I want to be when I grow up, and you kinda have to know one to choose the other."

Eric looked deep in thought. "I get it. Almost all schools give you time to pick your major, but, yeah, if you want to go to the school that's best for, I don't know . . . architecture, then you have to know you want to be an architect."

"That's exactly it," I said.

Adrenaline raced through my chest—someone actually understood me. Bri and Teagan had just given me puzzled stares. Bri was going to get an MBA and be a businesswoman, like she had planned since she was a little girl playing with her mom's heels and laptop bag. Teagan was destined to be an engineer—she was all numbers and geek tech forever. But Eric at least understood the conundrum.

I started talking faster. "Technically, I could do liberal arts or whatever, but that seems like a waste if I get in and realize what I really want to do is computer science. And if I go to a school like Cooper, it's even harder, because what if I don't find a home in any of their programs?"

"You'd have to transfer," he said.

"Which would be like starting all over again." I pressed my palms against my bare knees. "I know it sounds like 'oh my God, this diamond crown is so heavy,' but going to a school like Carver makes it feel like I have too many choices. It's like this long hallway is in front of me and all these doors are open. But then everyone expects me to have no trouble choosing the correct door because I'm a straight-A student. We're supposed to succeed. But the things is: You can only walk through one door. And you have to pick the right one. The problem with that is, I don't have a passion for anything. I'm good at a lot of things and great at nothing. So I'm stuck at the start of the hallway watching people like Bri blissfully choose a door. I don't expect you to relate, you've chosen a door too. You've known you've wanted to be pediatrician your whole life."

Eric looked to the side.

"Wait. You don't want to be a doctor?" I fully turned in my seat to face him, my eyes wide, totally in shock. He could've torn his face off and revealed he was a cyborg and that wouldn't have surprised me as much. Eric not wanting to be a doctor, though . . .

He shook his head. "No, I . . . I do."

I made a face at him, arching my eyebrow as high as it could go.

"It's complicated."

I blinked twice.

He sighed. "It is what I want to do, or at least it was what I wanted since I was a toddler. I've always been interested in anatomy and physiology, and of course I wanted to be like my dad."

"I know," I said. "You were a doctor for, like, every Halloween. It was so uninspired."

He rolled his eyes. "We can't all be something cool and artistic every year like you."

He was right—my costumes were the best. My dad and I would brainstorm for months and then my mom would veto some as too over the top or too unsafe. Like the time I wanted to be Katniss Everdeen with her costume that was on fire. Mom made us settle for LED lights. Weak sauce.

"But, go on," I said. "What is it you want to do then, because I'm sure you know?"

"Football." He glanced down, away from me.

"Really? Like NFL?"

"No, I'm not good enough to play in the NFL, but I want to go as far as I can. And once that's over, I want to stay around football as long as possible, maybe as a coach, or trainer, or even a sports medicine doctor."

"Okay, what's the problem with that?" I asked. "If you become a trainer or a team doc, it's still a branch of medicine."

"For starters, Hopkins isn't a Division One school."

I didn't understand what that meant outside of the fact that not going to Hopkins would change everything for him.

"They have a football team, but the top talent goes to Division One," he added.

It made sense that Eric would want to go where it was most competitive. As annoying as it was for him to be the "Hero of Carver," he was, in fact, a great quarterback. Unfortunately, almost all his teammates played exactly like the nerds they were. Very often his throw would be perfect but the receiver would drop the ball. Or they'd catch it and then lose it tripping over their own feet. It was rough to watch, and I'd had to because Bri was a cheerleader and I was supportive. It's no exaggeration to say Eric was the only reason Carver was competitive at all.

"So the teams that play the college championship are all Division One?" I asked.

"Yeah," he said.

"Is UPenn Division One?" I asked.

"It is."

"Well, maybe you might get something out of this visit too," I said.

He shook his head. "No, I . . . I can't go to Penn."

"Too good for the Ivies? Or too worried about a restraining order?"

He rolled his eyes over to me. "Neither. I'm a legacy at Hopkins, and they have a great med school. That's where I have connections and where I should go. Jessica thought it was ridiculous for me to consider anywhere else."

Ah, so the perfect, salad-throwing girlfriend thought it was a bad idea. No wonder he'd put it out of his mind. But it wasn't like Eric thought he'd be the quarterback for the Patriots—he wanted to be a coach or a team doctor. Seemed pretty reasonable to me. And even if it was a low-percentage thing, so what? My mom had supported my family for years while my dad wrote. Because love was about encouraging someone's dreams.

"I don't think there's anything ridiculous about doing what you love, Eric," I said. "If you want to do it, you should."

"It's . . . I'm not like you," he said.

"Well, really, who is?" I brushed imaginary dirt off my shoulder. "Like me, how?"

"The hallway thing. You see it as having a line of doors all open to you. I see it more as steps building up to a destination."

"Ones you can't change?" I said. "Because it leads to only one spot and every step is locked in? That sounds suffocating."

We passed the sign for Camden and Philadelphia, and there were longer pauses between our questions and answers as the robot lady barked out rapid commands for turns and merges.

Eric wove us closer and closer to the campus, but when we stopped at a red light, he looked over at me.

"You don't know what it's like to work as hard as I do, to never lose focus, to stick to the plan, only to have you come in and uproot it all," he said. "Do you even study?"

"Kinda."

He sighed. "You're such a bad liar."

"Well, I study a little. But mostly it's to beat you. I'd easily get an A going in cold, but a ninety-five doesn't cut it when you get a ninety-six."

"So you get a hundred. It's the most obnoxious thing in the world."

"Right back at you," I said. "I'd be happier as the solo genius."

"Would you?" His hazel eyes searched my face.

My mouth suddenly felt dry, my face warm, but I'd be damned before I drank another thing in that car. "I . . . I don't know. Wouldn't you rather be a lone superstar?"

"No," he said. "Having a rival pushes you. History has had tons of rivalries and they've produced greatness, like the Space Race or Edison and Tesla."

The light turned green.

"You're Edison," he added.

I scrunched my nose. "He was an asshole."

"Exactly."

Touché.

CHAPTER NINETEEN

Kelsie's Log of Failure

FOURTH GRADE

"The first prize award for the Garfield Elementary School Science Fair goes to the most unique experiment we've seen in the history of this fair. We are pleased to award Eric Mulvaney Ortiz and Jason Gallagher our gold prize for their potassium pump. Second prize goes to Kelsie Miller and her wind farm."

—Mrs. Jackson, Principal of Garfield Elementary

Edison, my ass.

CHAPTER TWENTY

We finally made it to UPenn and parked on the street a couple of blocks from the main entrance. The university was right in the city, amidst road construction and one ways, so we had to circle to find parking. That was fine by me. The closer we got, the more dread built in the pit of my stomach. Would today be a triumph or an abysmal failure?

I checked my phone when Eric paid for parking and again as we waited for the crosswalk signal. No new messages. Part of me was beginning to resign myself to the fact that Bri just didn't want to hear from me. The thought made me want to crawl back into the car and go home, but I'd gone this far. Might as well cross the street.

We stopped in front of a red, white, and blue map of the school to the side of the campus entrance. The University of Pennsylvania had dozens and dozens of buildings.

"Holy shit, this is the biggest campus in the world," I said.

Eric shook his head. "It really isn't. Have you not toured any colleges yet?"

I hated that I had to crane my neck to look up at him when we were both standing.

"I went to Cooper," I said.

My parents had been more than happy for me to lie about virtually touring campuses as going to see schools cost money—gas, tolls, maybe hotel rooms if it was farther away. So I pretended like I'd visited a bunch of schools and they pretended like I was a good liar.

"Cooper barely has a campus. That doesn't count," Eric said. He pointed to the map. "UPenn is just this central road and everything is off it. It's a city campus, so it can't sprawl as much as a college in the middle of nowhere. These are all the graduate schools, so we don't need to bother looking there. The freshman dorms are over here. Jessica's in Hill College House, but we need to find the undergraduate admissions building first."

"Why?"

He squinted at me. "Because we registered for a tour."

I scrunched my nose, making my sunglasses shift. "We're going on that?"

He gave me a "seriously?" face and hand gesture.

I shifted in my sandals. "It's dawning on me that I'll look like a stalker if we're in the same group as Bri." My heart thundered in my shirt at the distinct possibility of her being weirded out.

"You're just realizing that now?" He looked around. "Now?"

"I'd thought it was a front."

He tipped his head back with a noisy exhale. "Look, the odds are very low we'll be in the same group, but the point is to find her, right?"

Reluctantly, I nodded.

"The tours may pass each other since the campus isn't that big," he said. "I've seen that happen at Hopkins."

Okay, passing her wouldn't be so bad, even if I'd have to do some kind of fake "wow, what a coincidence!" type of thing.

I took a deep breath. "All right."

"You're good?" He seemed skeptical.

"Yeah, let's do this," I said.

We found the admissions building on the map and headed down the tree-lined road. The oaks looked like they'd been there since William Penn. Everything was stately brick and stone. Exactly what I'd expected from an Ivy.

Eventually the brick pavers led us to the visitor center. We checked in for our tour and happened to be the only two teens without chaperones. Prospective genius students plus overbearing parents were lined up along the gray stone steps. Luckily, Bri wasn't there when we arrived. I wondered if she'd come alone. She hadn't mentioned in her posts or comments whether or not Elaine was with her, and Elaine only posted about work things. Not that I'd checked or anything.

I just happened to know she was proud of her finance team for surpassing their goals this quarter.

Okay, fine. I'd looked.

At exactly two thirty, an entirely too chipper person in a UPenn shirt and khaki shorts whistled at our group. He said his name was Jeff and to follow him!

So began our grand tour. Bri was not, in fact, in our group, and I was relieved, but then the reality sank in: it would be much, much harder to find her.

We followed Jeff around. He walked backward nearly the entire time and was the human equivalent of a bouncing exclamation point, but Eric didn't seem to notice. He marveled at the sculptures like we were there to take in the sights.

"This campus is pretty nice," Eric said. "Not what I expected when I saw it was right in the city. And even Jessica's Insta doesn't capture the feeling of being here."

"It's weirdly still and quiet," I said.

"There's a calmness to it even though it's in Philadelphia. It's nice." Eric gazed at the trees, and I remembered he'd at least looked into playing football for them, so I let him be.

I kept my eyes peeled for both of us while we went in and out of the highlight buildings, from a sample classroom to the dining hall to passing by the official campus bookstore and merch outlet.

No sign of Bri or Jessica.

The tour ended, taking us right back to the admissions office at 3:30 p.m. Jeff, of course, gave some nice closing about seeing us in the fall. I looked at Eric and noticed a light in his eyes that I'd only seen when he was talking about Jessica.

He loved UPenn.

"So, what did you think?" I asked.

"It was okay," he said.

Oh, so we were going to downplay it. Cool, cool.

"Yeah," I said. "What's the plan now?"

"Huh?"

Eric seemed mentally at war with himself over the path he'd chosen as a two-year-old versus what he wanted now. But I didn't have time for that because with every blond who wasn't Bri, I got a little more discouraged.

"For finding them," I said. "In case you haven't noticed, we didn't achieve our goals for the day yet."

I did a little jazz hands motion and he shook his head like he was remembering where he was.

"Well, we can wait around for a while," he said. "We know the route the tours take now. I'm sure they're all the same. If Bri's in a later tour, we'll see her."

Ugh, it was so smart. I realized we should've left at seven in the goddamn morning as he'd suggested. We would've been at the campus for the 11:30 a.m. tour and could've staked out the route all day. Thankfully, I knew Bri wasn't a morning person. And since she was flying in from the West Coast, it would've been even harder for her to get up. My thought was she wouldn't have rolled out of bed before noon and she'd have to eat and shower and take an hour to do her hair, so she probably scheduled a two o'clock or later tour.

We camped out at a table and chairs near where the tour had begun and watched people go by. I anxiously scanned the three o'clock tour, which had just come back, but she wasn't there. She also wasn't in the three thirty.

Eric and I made polite, meaningless conversation to pass the time. Neither of us was particularly engaged because we were both scanning for our exes or checking our phones. But I had to admit, it was serene on the campus.

The last tour of the day was at four, and Bri was a no-show for that, too. I sat back in my seat after the tour group passed and sighed. I'd kind of hoped everything would fall into place and it hadn't. So how could I find her?

"Oh God," Eric said.

"What? You see Bri?" I bolted upright in my chair, looking all around.

"No, it's . . ." He turned his phone at me. Jessica Lovelace had looked at his Instagram Story.

My stomach churned, but it was probably because I'd had a triple bacon burger for lunch. "That's good."

"You were right," he said. "I can't believe it. It worked!" He tapped on the table, barely able to contain himself.

Normally, I loved being right, but his joy seemed premature. It wasn't like she'd texted back or anything. Maybe I was just jealous, though. Once again, he'd been successful and I hadn't.

I forced a smile. "I'm glad it did."

He stood up. "You're the best. Now I need to find a florist."

"Why?" I said.

"Because I finally have an idea of what to do, and it's all thanks to you," he answered.

"Me?"

"Remember when you said we should come here with roses for them? That's what I'm going to do. Would you . . . would you be game to help me pick out flowers?"

"Um . . ."

I didn't want to, but I also didn't have any leads yet where Bri could be, and I didn't want to wait around on campus alone. Nothing could be lonelier than being at a busy college all by myself. Plus, he looked so happy and excited; his enthusiasm was contagious.

"Yeah. Sure," I said.

Eric found a shop on his phone, and with that we were on our way back to the BMW. He was almost vibrating with energy, and I tried not to be bitter about the fact that it had been the two of us on the way down but now it felt like there were three of us in Philadelphia.

CHAPTER TWENTY-ONE

We pulled up to the Posy Peddler, a small store on a fairly busy road a couple of miles from campus.

"So tell me again what we're doing," I said.

"I'm going to get Jessica fifty-six flowers." He held open the door to the shop and I nearly tripped on the threshold.

"Um, why?"

"Well, she looked at my Insta—" he began.

"No, why fifty-six? That's oddly specific."

"Oh, because we were together at football camp for fifty-six days. Well, she was helping out as an assistant to her dad and I was at the camp . . . you know what I mean."

I stared at him. "Yeah, it's not creepy at all to know that down to the day or anything."

Ignore the fact that I knew down to the hour how long it had been since Bri had spoken to me.

The floral smell was overwhelming as we walked around

the cramped shop. It wasn't a large place, but it was packed with flowers so we had to cruise slowly to take it all in. There was someone working at the counter, but he was on the phone and utterly uninterested in helping us.

"You don't forget the day you meet someone like Jessica," Eric said. "Or the day you lose her. But she liked to point out the time to me. She said it was day fifty-six the morning I left camp. Do you think I should add more since it's been longer now?"

"No . . . I . . ." I didn't want to tell him his relationship had likely ended on day fifty-six. "I think that number has more meaning."

"Which do you think?"

I turned and looked at him. "Doesn't she have a favorite flower?"

She seemed like someone with a favorite flower, a favorite everything.

Eric pursed his lips. "I'm not sure. I got her three roses for our first date because we'd known each other for three days, but I think they're too pedestrian, you know?"

Ugh, only Carver kids used the term "pedestrian" in casual conversation. Still, I nodded.

"Yeah, it has to be something special," I replied. So the normal suspects were out: roses, tulips, carnations. Great—super easy.

"What's your favorite flower?" he asked.

"I . . . I don't have one," I said. "I've never gotten them."

"No guy's ever given you flowers?" From his face, you'd think it was impossible.

"As much as they're all beating down my door, somehow no," I said.

"A lot of guys have liked you," he said. "What do you think of lilies?"

I wrinkled my nose and we kept browsing.

"That is a pleasant fantasy," I said. "Hydrangeas?"

He touched the ones I pointed to. We were, like, four feet into the store and kind of on top of each other.

"I've seen them on her Insta, but they don't feel distinctive," he said. "And, no, I'm not kidding. I've heard guys talking about you, especially ones who don't know you."

I took a sprig of a wooden stem and hit him with it. That, of course, made the guy behind the counter notice and frown. I put it back and raised my hands like I'd never touch anything again.

"I'm serious," Eric said. "Okay, that came out badly. Dahlias?"

I looked at the flowers. They were beautiful, but each one was, like, ten bucks. "They're all right, but fifty-six of them will be a fortune. And what did you mean?"

"I mean that guys who know you at school are intimidated, but guys who just meet you like you."

I rolled my eyes. "Yeah, I'm real intimidating at five-one."

"I didn't mean height," he said. "I'm not seeing anything. Maybe we should go with the hydrangeas. Or try another store?"

"What are we even talking about?" I dropped my hands and they slapped against my sides.

Eric stopped browsing and faced me. "There are guys at Carver who'd ask you out, but they're afraid because you're so smart and so . . . you."

I arched my left eyebrow. What kind of fragility nonsense was this?

"No one likes rejection, and you don't seem interested in dating anyone," he said. "You don't flirt at all. Or wear getups like this or go to parties. Yeah, I said 'getup' again and you're good with it."

I let myself absorb what he said. He was right . . . kind of. Intelligence was the capital at Carver, and in that hierarchy, I was queen. If that was intimidating to someone, I didn't want to bother with them anyhow. And, truly, I wasn't interested in dating anyone, but I did suddenly feel robbed of at least being given flowers.

"If I wore shorts, I'd be asked out more? Come on," I said.

He shook his head. "No one can really figure you out."

"I'm quite the riddle," I added.

"You are," he muttered.

I was about to ask him to explain, but we came to a display of gorgeous pink peonies.

"Perfect," we said at the same time.

Eric smiled. He took the whole bucket up to the counter, and I was left with a strange wish that they were for me.

CHAPTER TWENTY-TWO

Fifty-six was a lot of goddamn peonies. We had to go to three different flower shops, and I'd decided not to notice how much Eric spent on the flowers and vases. Or how long it was taking. Every minute he used writing out a three-phase card system was a minute we weren't looking for Bri. I'd groaned when he tore up a draft, but I'd used the time to stalk Bri's social media pages, and very unusually she hadn't posted anything, so I didn't have leads anyhow.

When we got back to the UPenn campus, he took three vases and I grabbed the remaining two. Did I mention that flower arrangements were ridiculously cumbersome when walking? We'd parked as close as we could, but we were still two blocks from Hill College House. I was huffing, juggling pollen and petals, and trying not to spill the water. I'd agreed to help, so I was honor bound to get these to Jessica.

By the time we reached her dorm, it was six thirty, which

seemed like a reasonable time for her to be in her room after classes and before dinner.

There was a long ramp that led up to the entrance. The doors to the dorm, of course, automatically locked. We stopped at the end of the ramp and Eric stood off to the side.

"Now what?" he said.

"Now we go to her room," I said.

"But . . ." He shifted his weight from foot to foot.

"Don't you know her room number?" I asked.

"Yeah, but we can't get in without swipe cards. Maybe we should try later or . . ."

"Eric, I'm holding two dozen peonies that aren't for me. We're doing this," I said.

His brow wrinkled. "How?"

"You can't be serious. Just follow me, my God."

Someone in shorts and a Big Bang retro tee walked up to the door and swiped his card. The door unbolted with a snap and he pulled it open.

"Hey, hold that!" I yelled out.

The guy somehow heard me over his earbuds because he stopped the door from closing with his foot and threw it open wider.

"Thanks, man." I smiled. He nodded and walked away.

I held the door for Eric.

"I can't believe security is so lax." He actually looked troubled, with a lined forehead.

"It's a college, not Fort Knox, and we're nerdy teens with,

like, five dozen flowers. What are we really going to do?"

We passed a lounge full of cheap, ugly couches and end tables. They'd had similar stuff at Cooper. Did every school shop at the same hideous furniture warehouse?

"What room is she in?" I asked.

"Four twenty-one," Eric said.

"Okay, let's find the elevator," I said.

"I mean, we could take the stairs if . . ."

He turned and looked at my face. I shook my head trying to resist the urge to murder him. I was not about to walk up three flights with all these flowers.

"Yeah, elevator," he said.

We found it and got in. Eric was oddly quiet and jittery once the doors closed. The elevator smelled like old takeout, every surface was questionable, and it moved so slowly that I had the time to think about standing there with flowers for Jessica as she opened the door. I'd go from tempting replacement to Eric's little sidekick in seconds. I wasn't sure what exactly had gone wrong in my life to lead me to this. It didn't really matter because I was in too deep to back out. But it was something to discuss with my future therapist.

When the elevator finally reached level four, Eric stepped out and followed the numbers down to 421. We found it and he straightened his posture, smoothed his hair, and knocked on her door.

My fingertips went cold with dread and I held my breath, but there was no answer. He looked confused, but he knocked a second time. We listened at her door for any sound, but her room was silent. She wasn't there.

"What's the plan?" I asked.

"I . . . I'm not sure. This isn't how I'd pictured it," he said.

"Do you want to . . ." I gestured back to the elevator with my head. I didn't relish the idea of returning to the car with the flowers, but it didn't look like there were a lot of options.

"No, no, let's leave them here," he said.

Relieved, I put mine on the floor. Eric arranged and rearranged the five vases against her door, so the three flowers with cards were in the front and in order from left to right. It took way longer than it should've, because Eric and his perfectionism had to get them just right. Eventually, he was done.

"Well, that was a raging success," I said as we got back into the elevator. "We just flower bombed her doorway."

"It's the first step," he said.

"Do we set up shop in front of her dorm and wait?" I asked.

He shook his head. "No. I think we look for Bri."

"Are you sure?" I was a little surprised that he didn't want to sit on a bench by her residence hall. Although staking out her place did sound a touch aggressive.

"Yeah," he replied.

We got out of the building, and I pulled out my phone and texted my mom that we'd be late because we were going to sit in on a class and get dinner after. She messaged back with a quick okay. And a second follow-up: "Be good."

Honestly.

Eric leaned against the railing at the end of the ramp and checked his phone. After he put it away, he looked defeated for the first time.

I looked up from my screen and tilted my head at him.

"I . . . I guess I'm anxious for this to be over," he said.

"Over how?"

"Resolved one way or the other," he said. "The worst thing about Jessica not talking to me was that our whole relationship was left unfinished. But she'll definitely see the flowers and either she'll realize what we have and contact me, or it'll be done."

He ran a hand over his face; his reaction wasn't what I'd expected. He seemed . . . resigned. It was so different from the energy he'd had when he was trying to convince me to go on the trip or even on the way to the flower shop. What had happened to make him give up on her so easily?

"She'll love it," I said.

He smiled slightly. "She's a fan of big romantic gestures and driving all this way to give her flowers has to be one."

"I think it is," I said.

He nodded twice and pulled out his phone again. "Well, look at that . . . we're in luck."

My heart clenched. Jessica had messaged him and they were going to live happily ever after.

"Bri just posted," he said.

What???

I scrambled to open Instagram on my own phone and there it was. She'd posted a picture of a fancy-looking dinner, complete with a bottle of wine. So her mother must've come with her. Bri was seventeen. She wasn't going to order a bottle of red at dinner, but Elaine was exactly the type of parent who'd allow her daughter to have a glass with her. My mom would've sooner given cabernet to the cat.

Hope flooded through me as I read her post. She'd shout out the restaurant and we could race over there, except I read to the end and there was no location.

"It doesn't say where she is, though," I said, frowning. I kept staring at the picture like if I looked or scrolled hard enough, it would reveal the name, but no such luck.

"Well, let's take in the clues," Eric said. "It's outdoor and it's fine dining. How many of those could there be around here?"

"They could be anywhere in Philadelphia though," I said. "Just because she came to see the school doesn't mean she's staying right here unless . . ."

I opened Elaine's Facebook once more and there it was. A check in at the Inn at Penn and a selfie of her and Bri with some humble gibberish about raising a future alumna. Because of course she tried to look like a good mom on Facebook. That site was built for old people bragging about lives they didn't really have.

I'd thought she might stay at the Ritz or something, but I should've known that they would've chosen the Inn at Penn. Elaine had gone to Wharton, the business school. That was why Bri was so fixated on going there. She wanted to be just like her mom.

I had no idea why.

"She's staying at the Inn at Penn, so let's head in that direction," I said. "It's on Walnut Street. So I bet they just walked to dinner. We can check the places nearby."

"Look at you, upping your stalker game," Eric said with a smile. He pushed himself off the railing and came closer.

"Have to compete with you for the crown," I said.

I bridged the distance between us and put my finger on his chest.

Too close. Way too close. I took a very large step backward.

"Let's go," I said.

I took off in a random direction to get away from the third goddamn spark. Of course it was the wrong way. Eric waved me in the correct one. The one I hoped led to Bri.

CHAPTER TWENTY-THREE

I'd like to say we didn't slowly stroll by a bunch of random, fancy restaurants Eric had found on Yelp, but I'd be lying. We peered into windows and scanned tables, making a large number of people uncomfortable.

Note: I still didn't have a clue what to say if I actually saw Bri, but it turned out I didn't have to worry, because we couldn't find her.

The problem was, although I knew Bri and her habits, I didn't know Elaine well enough to say if she was the type of person willing to Lyft to a restaurant despite there being good ones right by where she was staying. I got the feeling she would. And even though Bri had posted their meal, they could've eaten early and been done by now. My point being, the Instagram post had given us false hope and a red herring on direction.

We were about to double back and try again when we

came to a barbecue place that smelled really, really good.

"Are you hungry?" Eric asked. We paused in front of the outdoor tables.

"Starving," I said.

"Let's dip in then. We can eat quickly and continue our hunt right after dinner. Maybe Bri will post something more specific later."

It seemed as good an idea as any since I'd had zero success so far.

All the outside tables were taken at Baby Blues BBQ, so Eric and I were escorted farther inside. The hostess put us at a small table for two against a wall.

Eric stood behind a chair and looked at me.

"What?" I asked.

He gestured to the seat, pointing down with his finger. I slowly came to understand he was pulling out the chair for me. My dad did that for my mom a lot, but a guy had never done it for me because I'd never been on a date. This wasn't a date, though. Eric was just being polite.

"Oh, right, right," I said.

I plopped into the seat and he pushed me closer to the table, but I dragged my sandals so my legs kind of got stuck. I knew this was a manners thing, but I didn't understand why.

He shook his head and sat across from me.

I opened the menu as the waitress came to take our drink order. I got sweet tea and Eric stuck with water. The waitress returned scary quick with our beverages, and I pored over the prices, doing some math in my head.

The chicken sandwich was the cheapest, but it didn't come with anything. The platters came with two sides but were more expensive. But the platters were less than adding sides to the sandwich. The problem was, I didn't have more than twenty bucks to blow on dinner. I'd worked all summer as a hostess, but I'd already stopped. My parents didn't want me working during the school year because Carver was a full-time gig and then some, so I had to make the summer money last. But I was not about to admit to Eric that I was too broke to afford BBQ in Philly, so a few dollars extra to avoid that embarrassment would have to be okay. I hoped the next summer I'd be able to waitress and make real money.

"What are you thinking?" Eric asked.

Too many things.

"Not sure yet. You?" I said.

"Either the brisket or baby back ribs platter. Deciding on sides," he said.

Both were more than twenty dollars before taxes and tip. But that kind of thing probably didn't matter to Eric, even though he didn't work. Bri never thought about prices when we were out either. She'd often grab the whole check when we got meals together. I was both grateful for that and a little ashamed by it.

"You look like you're cramming for an exam," he said.

"Big moves, here," I said. "Maybe the chicken sandwich, not sure."

"Oh, dinner is on my dads, by the way," Eric said.

I looked up from my masters in barbecue pricing. "No."

He unlocked his phone and turned his screen to show me the message from Dr. Ortiz telling him to take me to dinner as a thank-you for my company on the trip.

I wouldn't take charity from Eric, but it was different having a directive from a parent. My parents offered to feed everyone who came through our door too. So I looked at the menu again, this time without intense math.

"I think I'll get the pulled pork platter," I said. "I was between that and the sandwich."

It wasn't a lie. Not exactly.

"Sides?" Eric asked.

"Well, who can turn down mac and crack?" I said. "Probably fried okra, too. You?"

"I'm thinking the grilled veggies, maybe coleslaw," he said.

"Seriously? It's like you looked for the worst choices." I smacked the menu. They had hush puppies, sweet potato fries, regular fries . . . all of those were better than grilled vegetables. What was wrong with him?

"I'm supposed to hit nutritional goals," he said matter-of-factly.

I raised my eyebrow as high as it would go. "Hey, they have a Caesar salad, should we get that?"

He balled up the straw wrapper, threw it at me, and hit me right at my clavicle. It fell into my cleavage and Eric's eyes watched it drop. He then proceeded to look anywhere but at me. Unfortunately, the paper had lodged itself in my boobs and there wasn't a graceful way to get it out. I'd have to extract it in the bathroom later.

The waitress came back and took our orders and saved us from the awkwardness of that moment. Eric swerved on his sides and went for sweet potato fries and collard greens.

"So . . . ," I said. He finally looked at me. "How about those Jets?"

He smiled slowly. "They're as bad as ever."

"Yes, but at least the fans don't jump on top of folding tables," I said.

Eric was a Buffalo Bills fan, and the Bills Mafia had the inexplicable habit of dive-bombing folding tables.

"You don't have much to celebrate," he added.

He was correct. I didn't watch a ton of football, but I'd inherited the Jets' suffering from my ever optimistic dad.

I shook my head. "Low blow, Eric. Low."

"My apologies. I didn't mean to mock." He laughed and gave me a boyish smile.

There was something about his lips that was attractive and . . . what the hell?? Stop it, Kelsie.

I sipped my tea. "Eh, it wouldn't be the first time."

Eric tilted his head like he was waiting for me to say more. "It wouldn't be the first time I've mocked you?"

Which time did he want to talk about? I wasn't about to bring up how he pushed me off the balance beam when we were kids, because who even remembers something like that?

And I didn't want to get into overhearing him in Congress Park.

"You laughed during my salutatorian speech in middle school," I said.

To start, it was bullshit that I'd been salutatorian. We were dead tied for valedictorian because we both had one hundred averages. The school decided that the tiebreaker would be attendance. Frigging eighth-grade attendance. Eric had perfect attendance, of course, and I did not. In short, I lost out on being valedictorian because of Hanna. The little petri dish had brought home both strep and a completely gross stomach bug that year, and I'd had to miss a couple of days because she'd given me her illnesses.

But as salty as I was about the whole thing, it wasn't Eric's fault that our middle school sucked and had shafted me. It was his fault for laughing, though.

Eric's eyes moved rapidly as if he were reading the contents of his own memories.

"I don't remember doing that," he said.

"Okay." It was exactly what I'd expected him to say. Of course a moment that had mattered a ton to me hadn't even registered in his mind.

He leaned forward. "No, I'm not just saying that. I don't remember finding anything funny about graduation because Jay wasn't . . ."

He closed his eyes. After a long pause he opened them again.

"I'm sorry. You're right. I did laugh. It wasn't because of you or anything you said. I thought about the way Jay would joke around in assemblies. How he'd put on this face and nod along like it was all so serious. Your speech was good. Why did you think I was laughing at you?"

"I'd tripped over pronouncing a word because I was nervous," I said.

"But I wouldn't have laughed at that," he said.

I set my tea down. "Come on, Eric. Let's not pretend we've ever been friends."

He rested his elbows on the table, getting closer to me. "I know. You've never liked me. I just . . . I'm not saying everyone has to, but it's bothered me because I've never understood why."

I stared at him. What kind of bullshit was this? Why was he pretending to be wounded by the fact that I didn't like him? For starters, it wasn't like he needed more people to like him. Second, he'd gone out of his way to earn it. But I guess he couldn't fathom anyone not liking him, no matter what he did. And that was beyond infuriating.

"You're kidding," I said.

Right at that moment the food showed up, and we tabled the discussion in favor of really good barbecue.

But all I could think about was the last time we'd willingly hung out, four years ago, and the real reason I hated Eric Mulvaney Ortiz.

CHAPTER TWENTY-FOUR

Kelsie's Log of Failure

THE SEVENTH-GRADE INCIDENT

The important thing to understand about middle school is how frighteningly little there is to do. I suspected there was more going on for junior high kids in big cities, but not a lot. Add in the horror of having to be picked up and dropped off by parents, and it's not a recipe for cool success.

But one warm September day Bri and I had gotten ice cream at Ben & Jerry's and were aimlessly wandering Congress Park, the small green space in the middle of downtown Saratoga. We were eating our sugar cones when we ran into Eric and some of his friends. I recognized Eric immediately, of course. I didn't know the other boys, but they were all athletic and kind of cute.

Our friends merged and suddenly I was part of a cool group, joking around, making fun of things, getting nasty stares from adults. I was laughing with Eric, who I'd decided to temporarily forgive for pushing me off that balance beam. I was doing an impression of our social studies teacher, who had the bad fortune to spit when he talked. No one really got it besides Eric and Bri, but they were cracking up and everyone was having fun.

Because all the boys played football, we set up an impromptu game of two-hand touch in the park. Eric and I wound up on the same team, and he threw the ball to me. I actually caught it and ran it in for a touchdown. He met me in the "end zone" by the fountains and lifted me up and spun me around in celebration.

And it felt good. Special.

Everything that day had been great until I had to go to the bathroom. This seems to be a recurring theme in my life, but that time there were restrooms right nearby. I went up the path and leisurely made my way back, still in the glow of feeling like part of a group for once in my life.

Bri was off somewhere on her phone and Eric and his boys were talking when I walked up behind them. I was about to tell him I was back when I heard him say, "Oh, Kelsie?"

I paused and listened in, admittedly eavesdropping on their conversation. But curiosity had taken hold of me: what would he say about me when I wasn't around?

"Yeah, the Asian one," one of the boys said.

"Cut it out," Eric said.

"What's up with you?" another said. "She yours or something?"

"No," Eric said. There was so much disgust in his voice that

I physically took a step back. "Don't talk about her like she's . . . Do better. Talk to Bri."

That was all I needed to hear. I wasn't someone Eric would ever be interested in—he sounded ashamed someone would even think it. Bri was the better option. These were things I knew, but it was still different to hear him say them.

So I pretended like I hadn't heard, and Eric and his friends soon left. But I knew that type of hurt would never go away.

CHAPTER TWENTY-FIVE

Eric and I had been weird since dinner. He'd tried a couple of more times to talk about why I didn't like him, but I shut it down and he stewed. It wasn't surprising. Eric had always been a sore loser on the rare occasions I actually bested him.

The tension between us didn't get any better on the way to the Inn at Penn. We decided to scope out the hotel in case Bri wandered in or out. Jessica still hadn't messaged Eric, and he, of course, had an arsenal of excuses for the radio silence after I'd made the mistake of asking.

"Sorry, did you say something?" Eric said as we walked down the street.

"No," I said. "Did you?"

"No."

See what I mean? Tense and weird.

"What do you plan on saying to Bri if we do see her at the hotel?" Eric asked. "Have you thought about it yet?"

I sighed deeply. "I want to ask her what happened, why our friendship wasn't worth enough for her to even tell me what was wrong. She didn't give me an opportunity to fix it, no heads-up there even was a problem. There have been moments where I've wondered: why am I doing all this for someone who doesn't think I'm worth talking to? But, like we said before: I can't let this go. I'm just not sure I'll have the courage to say any of that if she actually will talk to me."

"It seems wrong that she'd just stop talking to you out of nowhere," Eric said. "Cruel, almost."

I stopped and stared at him. "I could say the same about Jessica."

"It's not the same. She's . . ." He paused and rubbed the back of his neck. "You're right. Neither of them is cruel. There must be reasons and that's why we're here, right? To find them and find out."

He held open the door to the hotel and we walked into a sitting area. To the left was a fancy large bar connected to a restaurant. The main entrance with the check-in desk was probably up the stairs. But there were couches and tables where we could sit and wait.

"Should we go to the bar?" Eric asked.

"Like we're middle-aged colleagues? They'll kick us out," I said.

"Okay, let's grab a table, then," he replied.

We wandered over and sat on orange couches set up facing each other like a booth.

Eric glanced at his phone. "It's after eight. We need to find them soon. We can leave at nine-ish and blame traffic, but any later than that and we won't get home until two a.m. There will be questions."

"Let me think," I said.

One hour. Jesus that was not enough time. I ran my hands over my face. Okay, I needed to think like Bri. What would she do? Knowing how likable she was, would she really come back to the hotel and stay in for the night? Maybe, to get a full night's rest if she had a tour tomorrow morning. No. I was thinking like me. Bri would've gone to campus after dinner and made friends with current students, if she hadn't already. She was always our social entry into groups and places because she had zero self-consciousness and could mesh with anyone. I was the one who'd tag along or want to stay put.

"What do current students do on Thursday nights?" I asked.

"Study," Eric said.

Yeah, Bri was not about to sit quietly in a library.

"Not helpful," I said. "I mean socially. Concerts, games, anything?"

"Greek parties, I would think. I've seen them on Jessica's Instagram."

Of course he had, but Eric's stalking might come in handy.

"Okay, let's go find one," I said.

"Really?"

"Yeah, the chances of Bri just coming back to the hotel to stay in with her mother all night are really slim. I think she probably found a way to get herself invited to a party. And even if we don't find her at one, maybe we'll run into Jessica. It'll be good for at least one of us."

"We're not students, though," Eric said.

"Do you have a moral qualm with crashing a Greek party?" I rubbed my temples.

"No. It's . . . it's fine," he said.

He didn't sound fine, but the clock was ticking.

"The only thing is, an hour isn't going to be enough time," I said.

"Why not?"

I stared at him. "Because zero parties get going before ten."

If social media was to be believed, Eric had been to substantially more parties than I had. Why didn't he know that?

"I see your point," he said.

"We need an excuse to stay the night," I said.

Eric's mouth dropped open.

Before he could say another word, a guy in a badly fitted hotel uniform walked up to us. He had a self-important air and smelled like onions. I could tell we were about to get thrown out and I cringed at the prospective embarrassment.

"Are you kids guests at the hotel?" he said.

"We're staying with Elaine Taylor," Eric said. He had all kinds of "can I speak to your manager" energy.

"Just . . . just making sure. We don't allow people to loiter."

Eric nodded once and went back to his phone. With that, the guy went away. Unlike me, Eric could act. Before sports had taken front and center in his life, he'd been the lead in an elementary school play. That meant he could also lie.

"Stay the night? At the hotel?" Eric said looking around.

"No, not at the hotel. Why? Do you have three hundred bucks handy?"

He frowned. "I'd have to charge it and that would blow our cover."

I groaned. "Obviously, we wouldn't stay in a hotel, Eric. I was being sarcastic. But in order to find them, we'll need to be on campus until midnight or so—maybe later. We can just stay up and out all night, but we need an excuse to tell our parents why we won't be home until tomorrow. And it needs to be good."

Eric looked thoughtfully into the middle distance.

"Let's say that we met student ambassadors who offered to let us crash with them to have a full Penn experience," he said. "Some schools offer overnights, but Penn doesn't have anything official. We can say it's the unofficial but common practice."

I mulled it over and realized it could work. It sounded logical, but above all, legitimate.

"You will need to tell my mom that," I said. "I'm a horrible liar. And I know she's going to call."

"No problem," he said.

He texted his dads and they were fine with it. But sure enough, as soon as I messaged my mom that we wanted to stay until the next morning for the immersive college experience, my phone went off.

"Momma Miller," I said, picking up the phone.

"Kelsie, what is all this about staying the night?" Mom asked. "You were supposed to have left after dinner."

"Oh, let her be," Dad said in the background. Of course my mom was on speakerphone. What was it with The Olds and speakerphones?

"I know, Mom, but we had dinner and . . . here, Eric can explain it better."

I handed the phone to Eric.

"Good evening, Mrs. Miller," he said. "Yes, we'd like to."

He launched into how we'd had dinner on campus with his girlfriend and how she knew some football players and they offered to let him stay in their quad. He claimed it was a great opportunity he'd hate to pass up, but he had promised to get me home, so he did understand if we needed to leave. Then he said I could room with Jessica to get the overnight experience as well. He was so persuasive and my mom liked him so much that by the time Eric was done, she'd basically agreed.

"Hi, Mom," I said, as he handed me back the phone. "So . . ."

"I don't know, Kel." I could almost hear her chewing on her nails the way she did when she worried. "Going down was one thing, but staying over . . ."

Dammit. Okay, I needed to break out the big guns.

"What was it you told me before I left?" I said. "I'm seventeen and in college soon anyhow?"

Take that, hippie cool mom bullshit.

She groaned on the other end.

"She's right," my dad said. Bless.

"Look, I need you to promise me that you'll be safe," she said.

I tipped my head back. "Oh my God, Mom. I'm about to toss my phone into the sea. I'm going to be staying with Eric's girlfriend. We'll be safe and fine."

"No drinking," my mom said.

"Is this a Persephone leaving the Underworld type of deal, because I already had sweet tea?" I said.

"Not funny," Mom said.

"It was a little funny," my dad chimed in.

"Way to have my back, Dad. Any more news yet?" I asked.

"Not yet. I'm trying to get absorbed in something new to stop thinking about it, you know?"

Yes, I did. That was something my dad said a lot. The only thing that helped him get over the angst of having a project out was to fall in love with a new one. It made rejections easier to deal with because he had something else on his mind. He'd already started the process of letting go.

"I can't wait to hear about it," I said.

"I'm serious, Kel," my mom said. "I want you to text me before you go to bed and when you wake up tomorrow."

"Okay, Mom," I said.

(My God, get me off this phone.)

She took a deep breath. "All right, I'm glad to see you interested in a school, baby. Have fun, but be safe!"

"Yes, Mom," I said. "Thanks. I'll see you tomorrow. We'll leave as soon as we're up and moving."

Eric nodded at me.

And just like that, we were now accomplices in one great, incredibly unsuccessful stalking caper.

CHAPTER TWENTY-SIX

We spent a while researching on our phones, trying to figure out if there was going to be a party and where it would be. After looking at Facebook groups, cross-referencing hashtags on Instagram, and figuring out which Greek members had all their accounts set to public, we found two. One was a huge end-of-summer, tropical-themed bash at a fraternity. The second was a welcome back night at a sorority. The latter seemed like a small get-together, but how many "just a few friends/ parents out of town" hangs had become huge parties in Saratoga? It was worth checking out.

Bri would be drawn to the campus event over a little house party. She loved huge concerts, clubs, anything where there'd be a lot of people. But it was also likely that she'd start at the Chi Omega house and then head over to the ATO party, fashionably late. And Jessica was being recruited left and right to join practically every sorority on campus, according to her Instagram, so she could be at either place.

We left the hotel around nine and started walking into campus to find the Greek houses. We stopped at the map, and it seemed like all the fraternities and sororities were on the east end and spread out over several blocks. It was fully dark out, but the paths were well lit as we passed academic buildings and a cute writer's cottage. My dad would've loved to have been the artist in residence. If he won Project Light, one day he would be.

Whenever we encountered groups of students, Eric did that bro-nod thing and they did it back. We'd have no problem blending in at the parties.

It was a quiet walk, but Eric wasn't checking his phone. Instead, he was staring over at my feet every now and then.

"What's on your mind, Eric?" I said.

"Nothing," he said. "But if you get tired, we can stop on one of the benches."

"Tired . . . of walking?" I asked.

"Yeah."

"Eric, it's walking." I gestured to my sandals and took two giant steps.

"I know, but Jessica would wear heels and her feet would get tired if we walked as much as we did today." He shrugged and we kept going down the lane toward the arched bridge in the distance.

"She wore heels to football camp?" I asked.

"No, of course not . . . well, sometimes. The camp wasn't far from Pittsburgh, so when we were done for the day or when we had a rest day, we'd go into town and she'd wear heels."

"What was the camp for?"

He stared dead at me. "Football."

I stared back. "I can't imagine why anyone wouldn't want to talk to you, Eric. I mean, what was the point, the purpose of the camp? Aren't you a little old for sleepaway camp?"

"Oh, it was a skills clinic. With quarterbacks they help analyze reads and stances, optimize throwing arcs, that kind of thing, but mainly the camp is set up to get looks from recruiters."

"Don't you have scouts at your games?" I remembered seeing some old guys in polo shirts on the sidelines.

"A few, but if you're from a smaller town, Division One doesn't tend to come out to recruit. A football camp brings the best of the best together, and recruiters can see everyone compete in one spot. So even players from bigger schools attend."

"So your dads know you want Division One, then?"

"No. They thought I was there mostly for the skills and competition. Plus, Hopkins also recruits there, so that was a selling point. Division Three schools can't give athletic scholarships, but they can cobble something together if they really want you. I think that's why my dads were happy with it."

I stopped walking. "Since when are they worried about tuition?"

It slipped out. I hadn't meant to say it, but it struck me as strange. His dads had more than enough for college. Weren't they deciding between a four-season room and a yacht?

Eric shrugged. "College and med school are expensive. They have money put aside for me, but anything I get in undergrad will help support me in med school and residency. Or help me buy a house or something later."

"A house? Are you serious?" I said.

"Like a down payment. I don't know."

A house. Eric was thinking about buying a house and I didn't know how I was going to pay for textbooks in college. I'd need some kind of work-study component at any school I went to. Which was a slap in the face. All these universities had huge, tax-free endowments, but they'd prefer to set up individual little indentured servitudes instead of giving stipends.

Yes, I'd made a resolution in the car to not resent Eric for his good fortune, but between him pretending to like me and now this house-down-payment shit, I was all out of zen.

I started walking again, my flip-flops slapping the pavers.

We took a few steps in the silence of the night, the only sound being my sandals angrily smacking against the ground.

"You did this at dinner, you know," he said.

I came to a halt. "Did what?"

Imagine all kinds of attitude squeezed into two words, and you'd have me standing on the campus walkway, crossing my arms.

"I was trying to have a real conversation about you not liking me, and you said 'you're kidding' and dropped it. I thought we were finally talking to each other. I thought . . ."

He trailed off and his jaw ticked, but he didn't say anything else. I found myself on the balls of my feet waiting for him to finish his thought.

"What? What did you think?" I asked.

He shook his head. "You're right, never mind."

He started walking again.

"Super-mature conversation," I called after him. I had to speed walk to catch up because he had long strides when he wanted to get away from me.

He spun around. "Oh, I'm the one who's immature? You won't even tell me why you hate me."

"Why does it matter?" I shouted, and stared at the sky. Aside from yelling at Eric, it was a nice night. "You really can't imagine there's one girl out there who isn't dying of love for you, can you?"

"I don't care about other girls!"

I stared at him.

He moved his hand like waving smoke away. "I care that it's you. We've known each other forever, and you've hated me for just as long."

"You started it."

"How on earth? Because I was the one person as smart as you in class? Is that what this is really about?"

Okay, so we were going to do this.

I shook my head. "Of course not."

"Then what?"

"You pushed me off the balance beam!"

Yes, I did indeed feel as ridiculous saying it aloud as I expected. But we'd opened the can of worms, might as well shake them all out.

He knit his eyebrows. "Sorry?"

"In second grade. You pushed me off the balance beam in gym and everyone laughed at me," I said. "That's how you started it."

He shook his head. "I don't remember doing that. I remember liking you. I remember being kind of clumsy when I went through my growth spurts. But, okay, look, whether I remember it or not, I'm sorry if I pushed you. It wasn't on purpose."

It was so easy for him to say sorry, to brush it off.

"Whatever. It doesn't matter."

I felt like the petty clown I was, and I really wanted the moment to end.

"It obviously does," he said. "But that was it? That was all that it took from when we were in kindergarten until now to make you dislike me so much? And you never said anything? I would've apologized years ago. God."

"That wasn't it. You asked what started it."

"Well, tell me the rest. You know I didn't mean to laugh during your speech."

I looked away from him. "Look, I'm not in a huge mood to relive all my middle school humiliations. I was lucky to have Bri then. I don't know how I would've dealt otherwise."

"Because I laughed? You're that . . ."

"It wasn't the speech, Eric!" I stomped my foot. I was all kinds of frustrated. About everything. All the unfairness in the world in general, but specifically how I didn't have Bri and instead was paired with Eric yet again.

We were full-on facing each other and yelling at this point. Aside from Hanna, I hadn't ever raised my voice at another human being. My mom would've put me in a wood chipper for yelling at Eric in public like a trash goat, but she wasn't available for consultation.

"It's what you said about me when we were in seventh grade," I said, lowering my voice.

He looked at me, and if he were an actor, an audience would've believed he had absolutely no idea what I was talking about. SAG Award material.

"The day we ran into each other in Congress Park," I added.

Same confused expression.

"Do you not remember that day either? You have pretty convenient amnesia, Eric." I rolled my eyes hard.

He put his hands out. "No, I remember that day really well. I remember it being one of the few times you were laughing and friendly. We even scored a touchdown together. It was a great day and one of the first after . . ."

He trailed off and I filled in the blanks in my mind. One of the first good days after Jay died. Guilt squeezed my heart and made me doubt my grudge, but still, even going through terrible shit didn't excuse him from being an asshole. I hadn't done anything to deserve it.

"I don't know where you're going with this, though," Eric continued.

"It's what you said about me that day."

"I didn't say anything bad about you."

I realized he still didn't know I'd overheard him.

I sighed. "I went to the bathroom, and when I came back you were standing there with your boys. None of you could see me from where I was on the path, but they asked you about me—if we were together—and you couldn't even hide your disgust. You said to talk to Bri because she was better. And while I'll concede the last part, let's not pretend that you ever wanted to be my friend."

His hazel eyes widened and moved rapidly back and forth. "I don't know what you think you heard . . ."

A denial. Of course.

"Can we not—" I said, but he cut me off.

"Let me tell you about that day."

"Forget it."

"Those kids were assholes. They weren't my boys. Let me tell you what really happened."

"No, I said to forget it! It doesn't matter," I rushed. Yet somehow the last syllable caught in my throat and I blinked back a tear. Because it had hurt. Because I was stressed and exhausted and very tired of people hating me. Because before that conversation, for a few hours in the park, I had liked him. And I'd buried those feelings under my hatred for him all these years.

I started to walk away from Eric again, but he took my hand

in his. I turned back and he stared at me. I was certain my eyes were glassy from the flash of pity on his face.

"You don't know everything," he said. "Actually, you don't know anything—"

I narrowed my eyes at him. "You're right. I don't know a thing. Whatever, Eric. Let go."

I pulled my arm with more force than necessary because he'd dropped my hand the second I said let go. Off balance, I flung myself back a step.

We continued over the high arched bridge to the Greek section in silence. All I could think about was the last time I'd said "you're right" to Bri.

And how I'd hurt my best friend who'd never hurt me.

CHAPTER TWENTY-SEVEN

Kelsie's Log of Failure

AFTER THE SEVENTH-GRADE INCIDENT

"Where'd everyone go?" Bri asked. She'd been on the phone with her mother. Her parents were finalizing their divorce and trying not to put her in the middle.

Note: they were totally putting her in the middle.

"I . . . They had to go." I'd been picking at weeds and sitting alone on the low wall near one of the fountains for the past fifteen minutes. I tried to blink back tears, but I wasn't as good at it then. A couple rolled down my cheeks.

Bri looked at me and her face dissolved.

"Hey, hey," she said in a quieting voice. She came around and sat next to me. Bri put my hand in her hand and her other arm around my shoulder.

We stayed there with me trying not to cry and her just being supportive. She didn't ask what was wrong or for me to talk about it. We sat still in the fading September light.

Finally, I wiped my eyes with the heels of my hands. "Eric is a jerk."

Her eyebrows rose and I could tell she wanted to argue, but her face returned to normal and she said, "Okay, then we hate him."

I looked at her and she smiled.

And that. Just that. Was everything. We loved each other unconditionally. We supported each other unconditionally. We were a unit. If one of us hurt, then both of us hurt.

We stayed in Congress Park for a few more minutes until I pulled the pieces of myself together again.

"Let's get out of here," I said.

"Absolutely," she said. "Let's get kettle corn up the hill and plot his untimely demise."

I laughed. "His violent, untimely demise."

"Obvi," she replied.

She popped up and put her hands out to help me stand. I took her hands and she yanked me to my feet. I kept holding on.

"I love you, Bri Bri," I said.

She smiled. "I love you, too, Kel. Forever and ever."

But maybe I didn't deserve forever.

CHAPTER TWENTY-EIGHT

It was an excessively long, silent walk to Chi Omega house accompanied by the sounds of our breathing and people having fun around us. I was stewing over Eric and his excuses, and he seemed mad too. Who knew what his problem was.

We took a wrong turn at a huge statue, but because we weren't speaking to each other, we weren't able to correct it quickly, so we had to circle back. Between yelling and the detour, it was after nine thirty when we arrived outside the rather stately sorority house that had Greek letters welded to a balcony.

"What's our move?" he asked.

I looked over at him, a little surprised we were back on speaking terms. But we did still have a mission. And while he'd laid down his flower booby trap for Jessica, I still had nothing to show for my Bri efforts.

The sorority house was lit up and there were clearly people

inside, but it wasn't exactly a raging party where we could've walked in unnoticed. We needed a Plan B.

"Let's go around and scope it out," I said.

He raised his eyebrows. "Casing the place?"

"Well, yeah, pretty much."

The sorority was very close to another Greek house, so we went into the narrow alley between them and peered into every widow. We tried to be casual about it—like we were just cutting through the property, but I'm sure it looked like we were peeping Toms to anyone paying attention.

I was about to give up on Chi Omega when I saw a head of wavy blond hair through the window. The girl was in a white tank top and jeans and had a bunch of bracelets decorating her wrist. Although there was certainly more than one blonde with jewelry in Philadelphia, it just felt like Bri. The little hairs on my arms stood up and everything.

"I think it's her!" I said in a stage whisper.

"Where?" Eric said.

"In the back room. Let's keep going. Maybe I can get a better look from the other window," I said.

Unfortunately, in our efforts to get around the building, we didn't realize people would be hanging out in the backyard . . . or that the building had a backyard. Or, well, a back space. There wasn't any grass, just rocks and concrete. A dozen students were chatting and drinking, but all of them turned and looked at us. The few guys playing cornhole only paused for a second, but everyone else regarded us in an awkwardly long silence.

"Sorry," Eric said. He slurred slightly, probably trying to seem tipsy. "Just looking for ATO."

"Oh," said one of the girls. She had reddish-brown hair and leaned on the railing of the metal fire escape. "You missed by one block. It's over there." She smiled and twirled her wavy hair, leaning over a little farther. "Need a beer for the road?"

Then she noticed me and her expression changed. She stood up a little.

"That's really nice, but I'm good," Eric said. "If my friend could use your bathroom, though, that would be awesome."

The girl's blue eyes shot over to me again and I did a little wave because, like in the elevator, I could not get away from being Eric's weirdo sidekick. I guess at the term "friend" the girl's opinion of me softened.

"Sure," she said. "It's in there on the left." She barely looked at me before turning her attention back to Eric as she came down the stairs. "Are you sure I can't talk you into a beer? We don't have cooties, you know."

He laughed and smiled that million-dollar smile, moving closer to her. I was stuck in the middle of their flirting and feeling an overwhelming urge to tell her what she could do with her beer. But Eric looked at me with a "what are you waiting for" face. And . . . oh! He'd said all that so I could go inside and check for Bri.

I shot up the back porch steps while the girl, Melody, continued to flirt with Eric. All the rest of the people had gone back to their conversations except one guy who was standing by the door. He opened it for me.

I smiled. "Thanks."

He looked me up and down quickly. "Thinking about pledging?"

"We'll see," I said, and with a flirty look over my shoulder, I went inside.

I barely kept my face together as I walked into the kitchen. As we'd seen from the alley, it was a smaller party and mostly girls—likely the sisters who lived in the house pregaming for the ATO party. A couple looked at me as I passed by a table laden with drinks and food.

"Just looking for the restroom," I said.

One pointed to a door near the living room.

I scanned the girls. There were maybe fifteen in the house, but none of them was Bri. Disappointed, I pulled the bathroom door knob at the same time someone pushed it open. I looked up and my heart almost stopped.

In front of me was the blond girl. Only it wasn't Bri.

"Oh, excuse me," she and I said at the same time.

"No, my fault," I said. "I got aggressive with the handle."

She laughed. "Well, no harm done."

Closer up it was clear the girl wasn't Bri. She had curly hair that had been tamed into waves and blue eyes, not Bri's light brown. She was two inches taller than Bri and looked like she tanned in the summer, whereas Bri stayed pasty year-round. Still, there was a familiar feeling from her.

"Are you Chi O?" she asked. "I don't think I've seen you at these things before."

"Oh, no. I . . . I'm not. You're Chi O?"

"Nah, I'm . . ." She looked up and to the right as if physically searching for the word. "Unaffiliated. But these girls can make a mean dip and no one ever touches the food at these mixers, so I'm kind of a regular crasher." She smiled and her energy was so similar to Bri's that it made me happy.

"I'm probably going to crash the ATO thing in a bit," I said.

"Ha," she laughed. "No girl can crash an ATO party. To crash you'd have to be unwanted, and they're desperate to get girls in. Maybe I'll pop over there later. Their parties can be pretty good—but listen: stay away from the punch."

"Noted. Well, I should . . ." I pointed at the bathroom.

"Oh, right, right. Excuse me a second time."

"Still fine," I laughed.

"See ya around. Nikki, by the way." Her bracelets jangled as she did a little wave.

"Kelsie."

Nikki wandered back toward the kitchen, probably to steal the dip, while I went into the bathroom.

I closed the door behind me and looked in the mirror. I smiled and touched up my makeup, fixing the eyeliner that had gone astray. I was proud of myself. For the first time in a long time I'd been friendly with someone new and met a cool person on my own. Maybe I didn't need to rely on Bri the way I thought.

After I went to the bathroom, I washed my hands and stared in the mirror again, only this time I didn't smile. Someone had put on Dave Matthews—Bri's favorite band. And I remembered the last time we saw them together.

CHAPTER TWENTY-NINE

Before Everything Went Wrong

SEPTEMBER OF LAST YEAR

Dad blasted "Ants Marching," a Dave Matthews Band song, in the Subaru on the way to the Saratoga Performing Arts Center.

"Come on, Kel! You have to get into the tunes," he said, loudly singing the wrong words.

I shrank in the passenger seat. I didn't know how it was possible for him to embarrass me this deeply, but success!

Bri and Teagan didn't mind, though. They were singing in the back, both big Dave Matthews Band fans. Bri's parents had loved them, and she remembered going to concerts when she was little and they were still happily married. Teagan insisted DMB put on a good show. They were okay, but since I liked going to the outdoor amphitheater for almost anything, I was game.

After an eternity of butchered lyrics, my dad dropped us off in the park. SPAC was a big venue that held tens of thousands of people for concerts like DMB.

We made our way through security and Teagan managed to sneak in a plastic flask filled with gin. After the Long Island Iced Tea incident, I was all good on drinking, but she mixed the gin with fruit punch and she and Bri drank it down while we scoped out spots. Anything outside of the amphitheater was technically the "lawn," but the grounds were everything from dirt to pavement to green grass. We'd brought a picnic blanket and found a grassy spot near but not too near a jumbotron.

A few minutes later four girls from Bri and Teagan's soccer team found us and the show started. I just wasn't feeling it. I wasn't drinking, didn't really like Dave, and I hadn't taken edibles like the girls on the team. A lot of people at Carver took various drugs to get them through. No judgment. I just wasn't one of them.

With Bri and Teagan mostly talking to their teammates, I was beyond bored.

"I'm going to go for a walk," I said.

"You okay?" Bri asked.

"Yeah, just restless," I said.

I got up, brushed myself off, and went for a long walk around the grounds of SPAC. Eventually, I felt my phone vibrate.

Kelsie Miller's Phone

Bri Bri Hoffman

Hey, where you at? Did you get lost?

Hey. I'm good. Didn't feel my phone

You coming back?

Yeah, on my way

I circled to where I'd left them, and the group now included half a dozen boys I didn't know. Teagan was flirting with three of them. One was trying hard to get Bri's attention, but she wasn't biting. She was bi, but preferred girls. And as soon as I appeared, he turned his focus to me.

This was going to be a long night.

"There you are," Bri said. She smiled at me.

DMB started a song called "Crush," and everyone stood and lost their minds. Well, except me. I just stood there.

Bri came up beside me. "Seriously, you okay?"

"I'm just . . . I think I'm going to cut out," I said.

My parents had a "pick you up anytime, no questions asked" policy. It was rare I used it, but it was nice to know I always had it. They didn't trust the safety of young girls in rideshares, so they were my Uber. Sometimes my dad showed up in a little chauffeur's cap. Then he'd have to roll next to me as I mock tried to get away from him shouting "No thanks, Mister!"

Bri frowned. "I wish you'd stay."

I glanced at the crowd of kids around us, weighing my options. I'd hoped it would be me, her, and Teagan. Or really . . . just me and Bri. But it wasn't and wouldn't be.

Bri's eyes scanned my face. "Is it too much?"

It was one of the advantages of having been friends for so

long: Bri could glance at me and know exactly what I was thinking.

"It's just not my thing," I said.

"Hold on. Give me until the end of the song." She took out her phone, rapid-fired texts, and then put it in her back pocket.

"No, no. You stay," I said. She was up to something.

She started singing along with the band, trying to make me dance with her. I laughed and gave in.

At the end of the song she talked to Teagan, but I couldn't hear them over the crowd roaring.

"Okay, we're all set," Bri said.

"What? No. You love Dave. You're not leaving because of me," I said.

"I'm not leaving." She glanced at her phone. "Come with me."

"What about Teagan?" I asked, hesitating.

"She said she's good staying here with the boys. Come on."

Bri pulled my hand and I followed her.

We walked out of the gates—so much for her not leaving.

"Seriously, Bri. Go back. I'm good," I said.

"I know you are," she said.

She had five inches on me and walked quickly through the parking lot. I had to nearly jog to keep up.

"Where are we going?" I asked.

"Aha!" she said. "There it is."

In front of us was her Audi. She hit a button and put the top down. Then she hopped up onto the backseat and sat perched half on the trunk.

"You've been drinking," I said. "You shouldn't drive."

"I'm not going to." She grinned. "My dad has the Audi because his Porsche is in the shop, so I wasn't sure where he parked it, but he'd texted the location. Take a seat." She patted the spot on the trunk next to her.

I eyed her skeptically. "What are you doing?"

"Hanging out with you, listening to Dave," she said. "Duh."

She smiled like this had been the plan all along.

Bri was right about one thing: we could hear every note of the concert from the parking lot.

I hopped up next to her.

"Bri, it's really okay. Go back in and see the show," I said.

"I've seen the show a bunch of times. It's better hearing it with my bestie." She leaned her head on my shoulder, and we sat up on her Audi the rest of the night listening to the band.

It was one of my favorite memories, but now, thinking back on it, I saw it differently. If it hadn't been for me, she would've been at the concert, not in a parking lot.

The cold reality was: she'd been willing to skip it for me, but I hadn't been willing to stay for her.

CHAPTER THIRTY

I put my hands on the bathroom sink as I realized that I'd never been the friend Bri deserved.

I could've talked to the boys who'd joined us at the show. I could've talked to the girls I kind of knew from the soccer team, but I hadn't put any effort into making friends since meeting Bri—so basically my whole life. Teagan was an exception, but she and I had basically been forced to be friends in order to continue hanging out with Bri.

When Seattle came up, I was too afraid of what my life would look like with Bri gone. Who would I be friends with? Who would I sit with? Who would I drive with to school?

The fact was, I'd clung to Bri too much. Maybe I should've cared more about what she needed for herself or . . . what would even be best for me. Maybe I'd held us both back.

I walked through the kitchen of Chi Omega, but there

was no sign of Bri, or Nikki, for that matter. Outside, I found Melody still shooting her best shot with Eric.

It wasn't working.

"Ready?" I asked.

Melody side-eyed me but smiled. "Nice to meet you, Eric. Maybe I'll see you over there."

"That'd be cool. Thanks again for the tip." He took a step back while still smiling at her.

I walked down the stairs and Eric gestured for me to lead the way. When we were on the sidewalk and out of hearing range he said, "Any luck?"

"No, it wasn't her," I said.

"You seem . . . are you okay?" He looked both ways and then we crossed the street.

"I'm . . . I'm beginning to wonder . . ." I said. "Never mind."

The bathroom revelation had made me forget that we'd fought on the way to Chi Omega and weren't quite on speaking terms.

We made it to the other side and he stopped and looked at me. "We don't have to talk about middle school. God knows it was a time I'd like to forget. But we're still on this trip. We said we'd talk to each other and you're definitely not okay, so what's up?"

I hesitated, but then thought about what he said. We were still stalker buddies and he did know both me and Bri. Maybe it would be good to talk it out.

"I'm just . . . I'm wondering if I was the friend to Bri that I thought I was. That's all." I wasn't sure why I added the "that's all," as that was a huge, earth-shattering thing.

Eric wrinkled his brow. "Why the sudden doubt? You guys have been best friends since always."

"I realized that I thought of her as mine, you know? She and I were a unit—like the right and left pieces of a 'best friends' necklace. We did things for and because of each other, but maybe I didn't allow her or myself enough space. Looking at Bri as half of a whole isn't seeing the full person, and I think I failed her in that way." I stopped and noticed he was staring at me. "Ugh, I'm rambling. This probably makes no sense."

I traced the crack in the sidewalk with my sandal, then looked at him again.

"No, it makes sense," Eric said. "I used to . . ." He shoved his hands in his pockets and drew a breath. "I used to think of Jay that way too—as the other half of me. I didn't ever have to deal with us growing apart because of what happened. But even when we were twelve, we'd already started to change. He'd started to mention that he couldn't do things the way I could. That day on the ice . . ."

He trailed off and looked into the night.

"Do you want to take a walk?" he said.

I nodded. "Sure."

We had to be close to the ATO party, but we walked down the street. I'd never heard Eric talk about that day. Not in person—nothing besides the clips from the police giving his statement about the accident. His dads protected him from requests for news interviews, and eventually it became this thing no one talked about.

We strolled along and I held my breath, straining to hear him, but it took a little while for Eric to talk.

"That day, the one . . ." He pursed his lips.

"I know," I said, hoping to ease him along.

"That day I wanted Jay to race me across the ice. He didn't want to because he said he couldn't run as fast as I could. And I . . . I dared him."

"Oh," I said. That dare must've been a lot, a metric ton to have on his conscience.

"The truth is: I'm the reason Jay died."

He stopped walking and his whole body deflated, his shoulders crumpling inward.

I stood there stunned for a second, then I vigorously shook my head. "No. Hey, no, you're not the reason, Eric. You didn't know the ice was thin."

He grimaced. "Yes, I did. That was supposed to be the thrill of it. Everyone knows the ice disappears at the end of winter. There was already open water in the distance."

I shook my head again and took a step closer to him. "You had no idea he'd fall through, though. You couldn't have known."

"Smartest kid in my class, aside from you, and I couldn't surmise it?" He smiled, but it wasn't a happy smile. It was an ironic, pained smile, the way I grinned when I talked about everyone hating me.

"Eric, that's different—"

"I was nearly to the other side when I realized he wasn't there," he said. "Do you know how far that is? I looked behind me and the ice was empty. Sometimes it's all I see in my dreams—white ice and a blue sky. I ran back as fast as I could, but if I'd kept pace with him, I could've pulled him out as he fell. Or maybe he wouldn't have fallen through at all. He would've gotten his shoe wet and we could've just laughed it off, but by the time I found him, I was too late. I killed him because I pushed him to do what I wanted."

"Eric, you didn't . . ."

Tears filled my eyes and he turned away from me. He didn't want pity. I was positive he'd had enough of it for a lifetime—the sad faces on teachers, on therapists, on other students. And no amount of pity had stopped him from thinking it was all his fault. So even though my heart ached, I focused on the logic side of it.

"Okay, look," I said. "Let's say you're right."

He startled and stared at me.

"Let's say he fell through the ice because you didn't want to see the differences between the two of you," I said. "But if Jay had been as strong as you, as fast as you, it still would've happened. Probably even quicker because he would've been heavier."

Eric stared at me with a slightly confused look on his face, but he didn't argue.

"The truth is, either one of you could've fallen through a

thin spot in the ice, and water that cold doesn't care about your forty-yard-dash time," I said. "Yeah, it was your idea to cross, and yeah, you dared him, but he started running because he wanted to. Because that's what you do when you're a kid—one person comes up with the challenge and the other clown does it. Kids have bad ideas every day and no one dies. You had no reason to think anything terrible was going to happen. Neither did he."

I sighed. It was such bad luck.

Eric was hanging on my every word, and it dawned on me that I was probably the first person to speak to him about all of this in years. The first one who also knew Jay, at least.

"It was just his time, and as unfair and shitty as that is, it's not your fault," I said. "You can't blame yourself."

He blew out a breath. "I beg to differ."

"Well, you shouldn't blame yourself. This is where the whole 'be perfect' thing comes from, isn't it?" I asked the question, but I already knew the answer. Things had gotten warped in his mind. After Jay died, Eric must've figured if he never did anything foolish again, if he never dared someone to cross the ice, he'd never have to suffer again. And if he achieved everything in the world maybe he could outrun the guilt of surviving.

He took his hands out of his pockets and shrugged. "I . . . I don't know anymore."

I tilted my head. This was probably part of the reason he wouldn't let go of the doctor ambition even though he wanted to play football. Football had so much built-in failure that it must've seemed foolish. Even for people who beat all the odds and made it to the pros, there were still teams like my Jets, so success was never guaranteed. But worse than failure was that Eric was eighteen and scared to fail. And I understood because, I mean, so was I.

That was it.

The realization hit me like a thunderbolt: I couldn't make a decision on college because I was afraid of failing. I wanted everything, including Bri, to stay the same so that I wouldn't have to face any of it. I wanted to freeze time and everyone in the same spot. But that was impossibly selfish.

The understanding knocked the air out of my lungs.

"I'm not going to stand here and say you shouldn't feel bad," I said. "Or that you shouldn't be afraid of failing. Because that would make me a total hypocrite. But, Eric, we're young. We make mistakes and we'll probably make a ton more. Even if everything that happened with Jay was all your fault, which it wasn't, you were twelve and made a mistake. Jay wouldn't have wanted you to be trapped thinking about it this way. He wasn't perfect. No one is. We're all messed up and doing the best we can."

Maybe that was the answer for me, too: to do the best I could. Maybe it would take me a while to figure out what I wanted to be, but I needed to try to attend the best school I could afford in the meantime. If I had to backtrack, then I would. Carver had made it feel like we needed immediate paths. They took a bunch of competitive kids and stressed the term "invictus," unconquered, with a level of pressure that could turn us all into diamonds, but there was no time limit on success.

Eric stared down at the concrete and then nodded. "Thank you, Kelsie."

I did some wavy hand gesture because I didn't know what to say.

"I mean it," he added.

I locked eyes with him and we drifted closer, like magnets pulling iron, a slow yet inevitable buildup. His hands were at his sides but his fingers opened, saying he wanted me nearer. We bridged the space between us. He smelled good. How come I hadn't noticed how good he smelled before?

We were inches apart when someone screamed "woo!" as they passed by us. We both leaped back, my heart racing in my shirt. I ran my hands over my hair. At the same time Eric folded his behind his head.

We stared at each other. He looked as stunned as I felt. The silence lingered and the echo seemed to hang in the night.

"So . . . uh, who's in the mood for a frat party?" I said.

He laughed and shook his head. We started in the direction of ATO, but I couldn't shake how close we'd come to each other. And how a part of me wished we hadn't been interrupted.

CHAPTER THIRTY-ONE

By the time we got to the large brick frat house, the party was in full swing and packed. As we walked inside, we were surrounded by so many tank tops, Hawaiian shirts, and backward hats. Was that even a thing anymore? Backward baseball caps? But we did kind of fit in. Eric looked like a dressier version of the frat guys, and no one could ever guess how old I was since I had a Korean ageless thing going on, but I was dressed fine enough to blend with the crowd. My normal sweatpants and oversize shirts would've stuck out, but looking like Bri had helped.

So, I pretended like we belonged and grabbed two beers from a literal trash can heaped with ice, heeding Nikki's warning about the punch. I went to hand one to Eric, but he put his hand up.

"I don't really drink," he said.

I gave him a skeptical face. "If there was ever a time to try, it would be now."

"I'll need to drive later . . ."

"Eric, you already know from AP Bio how quickly alcohol metabolizes. Do the math. You're fine with one. But, really, it's just to blend. You don't need to drink it. But how many people do you see here not drinking?"

He took it from me. I opened my can and started drinking an ultra-light but very welcome beer. I still didn't drink much post–Long Island Iced Tea incident, but I was okay with an occasional beer.

We scanned the crowd and then I realized it: it was going to be difficult to find Bri or Jessica even if they were at the party. There were people throughout the house and outside. There were so many rooms and so many potential places the girls could be.

"Should we divide and conquer?" I asked. We did, in fact, still have separate agendas, and I needed a little space from that moment outside.

Eric shifted his weight. "I don't know. It might be difficult to find each other again with all these people here. Probably better to stay together."

"Why don't we do this: let's each do a pass of part of the party, and then we'll meet back here? Can't be that difficult to find the front door again. I'll do the upstairs and you take the downstairs and outside."

"I'll take upstairs."

I knit my eyebrows at him. "Why?"

"Well, that's where the bedrooms are . . ."

I stared.

"I don't want anything to happen to you. Frat guys . . . I don't know, Miller. Just take the outside and meet me back here in twenty."

I laughed and shook my head. "Okay, I'll keep my phone on me. If you see Bri, text me. I'll do the same for Jessica. Text me if you find her, too."

"Hmm?"

"So we don't keep looking for someone we already found."

"Oh, yeah, okay."

We a hundred percent needed time away from each other.

With that, Eric walked up the stairs, and I slowly went through the first floor of the frat house. The music was good but really loud, and all around me people were idling with red Solo cups. I passed a lot of leering baseball caps as I scanned, peering into every nook and cranny. Just like at Fasig-Tipton, it was like I had a sign on me that said: Please look me up and down. A couple of guys said hey, but as it was clear I was searching for people, I was mostly left alone. I was somewhat flattered, but also I'd regretted dressing like Bri instead of myself. It felt like I had on a costume. I liked academic attention; other kinds unnerved me.

I made it to the messy kitchen, and there were obligatory, mostly empty chip bags on the table. Chi Omega had a much better spread. I stepped around people to get outside and onto the stone patio. The yard had a sand volleyball court they'd turned into more party space, and someone was grilling hamburgers.

I looked around for Bri and Jessica, truly unsure how I'd feel about seeing either, but instead I found Nikki. She was tossing a cup of punch off the railing and onto the grass below.

"Doing the world a favor?" I asked, walking up to her.

She laughed. "Yes, indeed."

She squinted then flung the empty cup into the air and made it into the trash can. She clapped, delighted with her success.

"I took it to be polite." She stared at the beer in my hand. "Glad you remembered the first rule of ATO parties: no punch."

"Is it drugged?" I asked.

"Drugged?" She laughed like I was hilarious. I felt super self-conscious about sounding like my damn mom, but Nikki must've thought I was kidding. "No, sadly, no LSD. It's just awful. It's grape Kool-Aid and grain alcohol with a ton of sugar to try to hide it."

"Yeah, that sounds disgusting," I said.

She nodded. "I made the mistake once last year. Fastest drunk and worst headache of my life the next day."

"So, you're a sophomore then?" I asked.

"Nailed it." She looked at me with an appraising eye. "You're a freshman from . . . Chicago?"

"No, well, I . . . I'm not from Chicago." I wasn't about to tell her the whole story of why I was down at UPenn. Instead, I drank more of my nearly finished beer.

"You look low," she said.

I blinked hard. "What?"

"Your beer. You look low. Let's grab another," she said.

I laughed. "Oh, okay."

I followed her through the crowd on the patio to a cooler. She hit the lid open like a pro and dug out two ice-cold beers, after searching for a better brand.

"Cheers," she said.

We each took long drinks.

"So, are you from . . . California?" I asked, squinting one eye. She had a laid-back surfer thing going on.

"Oh, so close. Small town no one's heard of in Oregon."

I skewed my face. "Is that close?"

She laughed. "It's West Coast, so good enough guess. But if you're not from Chicago, then—"

"Nikki," a guy yelled out. He walked up to us in a button-down shirt and shorts. He had a short beard, probably to make up for his weak chin, and he was sweating through his shirt from the late summer heat.

She groaned and frowned.

"Who's that?" I whispered.

"A TA," she said. She fixed her face into a pleasant expression. "Hey, Marshal."

She air-kissed him, and he pulled her into a hug. He and Nikki were around the same height of five-eight-ish. Nikki disentangled as gracefully as possible, but Marshal's hands had already roamed all over her back.

He was definitely older than us, but not by a lot, despite his thinning brown hair. I knew TAs were teaching assistants and usually students getting their master's degrees, so he was younger than my teachers in high school, but kind of old to be at a frat party. His watery eyes fixed on me.

"Who's your friend, beautiful?" he said to Nikki.

"Oh, we don't really know each other," she said.

It hurt for a second, but then I realized she was trying to get me away from him. Her blue eyes hit their corners, and with a slight tip of her head she was gesturing for me to start moving. I turned to leave.

"Well, then, let me introduce myself. I'm Marshal White." He extended his hand.

"Kelsie," I said.

I went to do a little wave, but he pulled me into a handshake with a hand on my wrist. His palm was sweaty. Gross. I tried to disentangle but got nowhere. He gripped my arm.

Nikki looked at me like she was sorry.

"I have to meet up with someone if you don't mind." I pulled my arm, but he held tight.

Nikki nodded along. "Yeah, you should try—"

"No, I insist you stay and tell me all about you." He didn't let go.

"Marshal," Nikki said. But she pursed her lips. Their whole interaction told me not only was he a TA, but he was her TA for a current class. Meaning: he controlled her grades.

I pulled back harder this time, but he didn't let go. He had my wrist in a vise grip. And instead of looking apologetic, he looked pleased as I tried to get free.

"Could you?" I said, struggling.

"Oh, no, I'm not letting you go," he said.

He laughed like it was a joke, even though it wasn't. Not in the slightest. His smile didn't reach his eyes. My shoulder and wrist hurt. He licked his lips. Nikki was visibly uncomfortable, and other people around seemed to be trying hard not to notice. But they did. He was a TA, and they were Ivy League students who cared deeply about their grades and futures, so they wouldn't intervene even if they wanted to. I was essentially alone in the crowd with this guy.

"I really need to go," I said.

He looked right at me and smiled. "Not until you say please."

I was so shocked, I just stood there.

"Please is only for when someone's being polite," a voice said from behind me.

CHAPTER THIRTY-TWO

If the deck at ATO had a tension meter, it would've cracked and broken. My wrist was still being held captive as Eric stood slightly behind me. He was visibly furious. The TA seemed confused, and Nikki's stare was volleying between all of us.

"Ah, look, the one I needed to find found me instead." I tried to stay light and make like it was all a big joke. Not because I found any of it funny, but because I wanted all of us to get out of it in one piece. Nikki, for her part, laughed.

Finally, Marshal let go of my arm. I had a red mark from where he'd gripped my wrist. I flexed it behind me, hoping Eric wouldn't notice, but when I turned and looked at him, he was staring down at my forearm.

"Is this some kind of game you play with girls?" Eric said. "Make them say please so you can feel like a big man?"

Okay, so we were not going to let this go.

"Who the hell do you think you are?" Marshal's sweaty face flushed red.

At Marshal's raised tone, nearly everyone on the patio turned like they could feel a fight in the air. Note: they'd been completely okay with ignoring him groping Nikki or not letting me go. But now there was a showdown.

"Think? No. I know who I am." Eric's hands were balled into fists, making his muscles stretch the confines of his sleeves.

Marshal looked from Eric to me and back again and nodded once to himself. "I didn't realize she was yours."

He smiled and put his hands up like he was innocent and in on a man-to-man joke. I couldn't have hated him more. So all of that was okay if I was single, but unacceptable if I was someone's girlfriend?

"She belongs to herself," Eric said.

"Oh, how postfeminist of you." Marshal snarled in a way-too-loud volume. "The sensitive brute scholar."

"We can take this over there if you want to get personal." Eric tipped his chin to the street beyond ATO and stared Marshal down.

He scoffed. "Kid, you have no idea who you're talking to."

"I don't really care." Eric shrugged but had all the danger of a coiled snake.

"I don't forget a face and I won't forget this," Marshal said, in a clear effort to dodge the imminent ass kicking.

He walked by us, hitting his shoulder into mine. It knocked me off balance but actually put my shoulder back into place.

Eric went to grab the back of Marshal's collar, and I struck his arm out of the way before he made contact. What the hell was he doing? If he swung at the guy, it would've meant all kinds of complications we weren't equipped to handle. We were underage drinking for starters, party crashers for seconds, and stalkers for thirds.

Marshal didn't seem aware of how close he'd come to death, and went inside. Eric and I faced off with each other.

"I tried calling you," he said.

"Well . . . I couldn't exactly reach my phone." I pursed my lips and indicated that my phone was in my shorts back pocket.

Eric closed his eyes for a long blink.

"I'm really, really sorry," Nikki said, coming closer to us. "He's such a bag of dicks, but no one can do anything about him."

"Why not?" I asked.

She sighed. "He's not only a TA; he's the son of one of the board of trustees here. He thinks it makes him immune, and the sad part is, he's probably right. He'll wind up a professor. I just know it. You were right to stop Muscles from doing what we'd all like to do. Hi, Muscles. You're fantastic." She smiled winningly at him.

He looked back and forth between me and Nikki, confusion changing into a small smile. "Hey."

"It was nice to see someone defend people around here," Nikki yelled.

A couple of guys immediately looked away, and I was glad she'd shamed them.

"Anytime," Eric said. He crunched an empty red Solo cup in his hand, taking his frustration out on the plastic. It was then I noticed the purple residue at the bottom.

"You drank the punch?" I asked.

"The Kool-Aid? Yeah, I had a glass," he said. "I was thirsty."

Nikki and I exchanged glances.

"A full glass?" she asked.

"Yeah," he said.

"It's grain alcohol and Kool-Aid," I said.

Eric's eyes went wide and stared at the empty cup. "Shit."

"I see it's kicked in already," I added, as Eric rarely swore.

There was a ruckus from inside the house, like people were pushing around furniture. I looked through the window and saw Marshal gesturing to the patio. He looked like he was yelling. Three frat guys were staring at us and would be coming our way any second.

"You guys better go," Nikki said. "Nothing good will come of this."

"Why?" I asked.

"No one likes Marshal, but as I said, he's powerful. Go vanish. I'll say you guys go to Drexel."

"Thanks, Nikki," I said.

Eric and I looked at each other. He grabbed my hand and we ran out of the party and into the night.

CHAPTER THIRTY-THREE

It turned out Eric was a terrible drunk. A terrible, large, off-key singing drunk, who was running sprints in an effort to metabolize the alcohol faster. When I made it to heaven, I'd have to ask Saint Peter why I'd had to endure this.

I sat on a bench by a statue of Ben Franklin or William Penn or some other old dead white guy. It was dark, so who could tell? But we'd run from ATO, back over the bridge, to the center of campus to get away from the Greek houses. I'd parked myself on the bench to catch my breath, but of course Eric still had tons of energy, even though he was also running in sandals. When he continued his sprints, darting back and forth in front of me, I rested my elbows on my knees and held my face in my hands.

"Eric," I said.

He was also still singing. Loudly.

"Eric!" I yelled.

He came to a halt in front of me.

"Someone is going to call campus police if you keep singing. And that someone may be me. You need to keep it down."

He crashed onto the bench next to me, breathing a little deeper. "You're right. Why do I feel like singing?"

"Because you chugged a glass of grain alcohol thinking it was Kool-Aid? Believing that at a frat party, at a college, they just had regular ol' Kool-Aid out for some reason?" I raised my eyebrow at him. We were geniuses who somehow had one (1) speck of common sense between us, and we had to take turns using it.

"It tasted like Kool-Aid," he said.

"Because it was. Aside from the alcohol part." I laughed.

He stared at me, eyes scanning my face.

He frowned. "You're not drunk."

"Nope. I had one beer and a sip of another before . . ." I trailed off and shuddered.

Even thinking about Marshal was unpleasant. I couldn't miss how he loved seeing me struggle. He was the kind of person who got off on that. He loved the power of it, the control. He was the worst kind of guy. Well, Marshal and Chuck were the worst kinds of people. I'd eventually realized the Chuck guy at Fasig-Tipton had tried to take advantage of me, but this was a different flavor of bad.

Eric, drunk as he was, seemed to follow my train of thought. "I could've killed him."

"Yes, I think everyone, including Marshal, realized that fact."

"No, I mean I would've killed him," Eric said. "At first I was upset because I looked for you and you weren't where we said we'd meet, but then when I saw you . . . I was . . . I could've killed him." He sighed and shook his head.

"I'm touched that you would've committed murder for me," I said.

He sat up and looked at me. "I'd stop anyone from hurting you."

Technically, I know that should've bothered me—the threats of homicide. It was hyperbole, but still, it probably should've been disconcerting. Instead, I felt . . . secure and flattered. The fact was, he had stopped Marshal. He was willing to stand up for me when no one else would. But the question remained: Why? This had to go deeper than road-trip-buddy loyalty.

"Why so protective?" I said.

"You really don't know, do you?" He breathed out a laugh and smiled to himself, leaning back on the bench with his arm across it.

"I don't," I said. "Enlighten me."

Okay, maybe I shouldn't have taken advantage of his drunken state to interrogate him, but I think I'd established that neither of us was on particularly high moral ground on this trip. And it was nearly midnight, we'd been wildly unsuccessful, and he was drunk. In short: I was curious and dealing with a lot of shit.

"You first," he said.

"Me first, what?"

He lowered his head then peered over at me. "Finish telling me why you don't like me."

Oh, *that* he remembered? Not the words to any of the songs he sang or the actual taste of Kool-Aid, but our conversation from before the parties was fresh on his mind?

"Eric . . ." I rolled my eyes.

"Finish the story and I'll tell you everything." He hit every syllable in ev-ery-thing in a singsong way. And, really, I might as well. He probably wouldn't remember what I said the next day anyhow.

"That day in Congress Park . . . you sounded so . . . disgusted by the idea of us being together, and I . . . I just never got over it."

He shook his head. "I don't understand what made you think that."

I stared at him. "Sure."

"No! I'm serious. I barely knew those kids. We played together in league football and my dads and my therapist had wanted me to get out and make new friends after Jay died. So I'd hung out with them that day, and they were ribbing me about you, but I didn't care about that. I liked you."

"You told them to talk to Bri because she was better than me," I said.

"No," he said.

"Yes."

He shook his head. "I wouldn't have said that because I've

never thought that. I . . ." His eyes went back and forth, then he sat back. "I know the moment you're talking about."

I threw up my hands and then slapped them onto the wooden bench. "Finally."

His jaw ticked.

"What? Why do you look like that?" I said.

"They said some messed-up things about you," he said in a low voice.

"Like what?"

He grimaced. "I'd rather not repeat it."

"Okay . . . what type of things?"

"Stuff about you being an Asian girl. I told them to do better. They shouldn't talk about any girls like that, but definitely not you. And they asked if you were mine or something and I said to talk to Bri because I wanted them to leave you alone."

I shook my head, not wanting to believe him. Not wanting to alter the memory I'd held on to for four years. But the thing was: I did believe him. I felt deep in my gut that he was telling the truth. I'd never seen him with those guys before or since. And what he said filled in the gaps in my memory. I hadn't heard the whole conversation and I knew that. But more than that, I could never get my mind around how we'd gone from teacher impressions and a touchdown to him talking about me with disgust. But Eric's disgust wasn't for me. It was for . . . them. He'd been defending me?

"So it was that, and then you thought I laughed at your speech, huh?" Eric said.

I nodded. "And competing against you for every tenth of a grade point and, frankly, losing most of the time since we were five."

He shook his head. "You didn't lose most of the time."

"Ha!" I barked.

"You didn't," he said. "We're tied now and continually deadlocked. In middle school they made me valedictorian because they felt sorry for me . . . because of Jay. I'd asked for us to be co-valedictorians. I told them it was unfair that either of us should have to be salutatorian, but they said no because there couldn't be two."

"You . . . you did?" I asked.

"Yeah. We . . . well, I, worked hard for that hundred average," he said.

"Nice correction."

He shrugged. "You're smarter than I am; you don't have to work as hard."

Quiet settled between us as I considered everything he had told me. It all made sense, as hard as my mind fought against it. From any angle I looked at it, he was telling the truth. He'd liked me this whole time, and I'd just been an asshole. Still, it was hard to change an opinion I'd had for years, even when the foundation had broken apart. Cognitive dissonance—what a shit.

We sat in the stillness of the campus at night. Wind blew across us, making my hair flutter, and Eric watched it on the breeze. The summer was ending and it would get chilly overnight. We were going to have to make a decision soon on whether to leave or to keep looking, but then I realized he'd never answered my question.

"Okay, if I'm so smart, what don't I know?" I said. "Why are you so protective of me?"

He smiled, amusement playing on his lips, but he looked away.

"No way, Eric. I told you. It's your turn." I nudged his shoulder.

He looked down at my shoulder and then into my eyes. We were sitting so close, our knees were touching. "You're impossible, Miller."

I laughed. "That's something I already know."

I ran my fingers through my hair, then put my hand back on my lap. He took my hand and gently turned it, looking at the underside of my wrist, which was still a little red but the mark was fading. He frowned.

"It's okay. It doesn't . . . hurt." I stumbled trying to swallow the word "hurt."

"It's not okay." He raised my arm toward his face. "Can I?"

"I don't know . . . sure?" I said.

He kissed my wrist.

My eyes went wide at the touch of his lips on my skin. Shivers shot through me and an ocean of feelings collided in my spine. I found myself leaning forward with my lips parted and then his mouth met mine. And it felt perfect. All the sparks had led here. From the one I'd barely registered when he picked me up and spun me around that day in the park, to the car, to the campus. It felt like a fire had lit in my stomach, a warmth I'd never known. This was what people talked about, wrote songs about, lost their minds over. I finally understood it.

Then all the alarm bells went off in my brain because he tasted like spearmint gum with a little bit of . . . grape Kool-Aid.

Wait. Was I really kissing Eric Mulvaney Ortiz when he was drunk and we were looking for his ghost girlfriend? Was he really kissing me? What the hell was I doing?

I pulled back and he opened his eyes. We stared at each other, breathing hard. I shook my head.

"Shit," he said.

"It's—" I was about to say it was fine.

"I'm sorry," he said.

That was it. That was all I could take.

I stood up, bolted from the bench, and ran in whatever direction would take me far, far away.

Kelsie's Log of Failure

TWO MINUTES AGO

Kelsie Miller's Phone

Bri Bri Hoffman

> Just kissed Eric.
> It was a weird mistake.
> FML

I ran until I found myself close to Jessica's dorm. If I bumped into her, it would officially complete this new messy low in my life, so really, I might as well.

I groaned and curled into a crouching ball. What the hell was wrong with me? How much did I want to torture myself? Enough to kiss Eric, who even though he apparently liked me as a person, was obsessed with someone else. Then, as if these thoughts weren't enough, I pulled out my phone. No response from Bri and she hadn't posted anything. I did have a million and one DMs, however, about Eric's earlier Instagram Story, including one from Teagan, which was just "???." I guess that was something positive, that she'd messaged, even if it was only to hear gossip.

But "???" indeed. He'd made the kiss seem so inevitable. As if he'd been into me for a long time.

I was a complete fool. And not even a good one. I was the

opening act for the court jester. A clown apprentice. His girl-friend or ghost girlfriend or ex-girlfriend or whatever hadn't contacted him even after receiving all those beautiful flowers, and he was drunk and looking for solace. And there I was, lips parted.

He was exactly like my dad, looking for a new project to try to forget about the one that was out to agents. To try to ease the sting of rejection. And I'd fallen for it. Hook. Line. Sinker. And the worst part was, I'd known better.

"Ugh!" I pulled my hair at my scalp and stood up.

My phone kept ringing. I didn't need to check—it was Eric for the seventeenth time. He'd been messaging and calling since I'd bolted. Running away was admittedly not my shining moment, but I couldn't talk to him. Because what I'd felt for him was serious and he was not. He was drunk. He was sad. He was in love with another girl, and I'd brought him here to find her. And what was wrong with me?!

It had been Eric this whole time. From the day when Bri and I were building a fairy house at recess in kindergarten and a boy had purposely knocked it over. Eric had swooped in and helped us put it back together. I'd looked at him and smiled and he'd smiled back. The competition against him, the way that I knew him so well, that feeling the day in the park when I thought he might like me too. That was why I'd been crushed by hearing him talk about me like I was nothing—I'd already liked him. But I couldn't admit it, even to myself. And then that crush had turned into poison as we continued to compete against each other in school. As he grew up and got even hotter, even more popular, ever more out of my league.

Now I'd kissed him, and I'd felt something real. And from the look on his face and the words that came out of his mouth, he thought it was a mistake.

He was my first real kiss and I was his drunken mistake.

Oh, rock bottom, at last I have found you.

But my night still managed to take a turn for the worse because when I looked to the left, Eric was running toward me. He was correct about the campus not being that large if he'd found me so quickly.

"Kelsie!" he yelled.

I did the mature thing and started running again.

"Kelsie!"

"Go away, Eric!"

I ran down the path in very much a not sports bra, boobs a-bouncing, with my hair down and my sandals smacking the ground. I had my purse under one arm but pumped the other going full speed because Eric was lightning fast.

"Will you just stop for a second?" he yelled.

"Leave me alone!"

And right at that moment we passed a campus safety officer.

I winced. Fan-frigging-tastic. Now we found one. Now. Not when Sweaty McTA had me in a vise grip. Or when his lackeys were going to chase us down. Perfect.

"Hey, hey, hey. What's going on here?" the guy said. He had a dark uniform on, making him look like an off-brand cop, and he waved his hands for me to stop. The lamppost light reflected off his bald head.

I stopped running and bent over to catch my breath, because Eric was so damn fast and in order to stay ahead of him, I'd had to sprint faster than I ever had in my life. Unfortunately, I wasn't much of an athlete, so I was left gasping for air right in front of campus safety.

Eric also stopped. I saw his big-ass sandals as I remained bent forward, trying to slow my breathing.

"Are you bothering this girl?" the guy said.

Immensely.

"No, no. He's fine." I was still sucking in air, but I managed to stand up straight, hand on the small of my back.

The security officer didn't seem a drop convinced. "Why were you running after her?"

"We got into an argument, sir," Eric said.

He must've still been a little drunk to give the world's worst answer.

"A friendly argument," I added. "We're friends."

"Then why you were running from him?" The officer raised a thick eyebrow.

"I'm very dramatic when I'm upset," I said.

I didn't break eye contact with him. He needed to believe me; otherwise, things would turn bad quick. Neither of us could afford Eric getting detained or arrested for harassment.

The guard narrowed his eyes at me. "What dorm are you in?"

"I don't live on campus." Because it wasn't a lie, I truly didn't live on the UPenn campus, he seemed to believe me.

"And you're sure you don't need to file a report?" He held out an arm for Eric to stay back.

"Seriously, we're friends and I'm drama. Didn't mean to disturb." I shrugged a semiapology.

"You both should be going if you don't live on campus." He put his hands on his hips and that was that. It wasn't a suggestion.

"Couldn't agree more. Thanks, officer. Come on, friend." I took Eric by the arm and walked back in the direction we'd run from.

When we were out of sight from campus security, I dropped his hand and we slowed down.

"So we can add almost getting arrested to the list of trip calamities," I said. "Are we ready to go yet?"

At that point I was willing to give up on finding Bri. I just wanted to get away from UPenn, Eric, and everything there.

"I still don't think I'm okay to drive." He glanced at Hill College House, and I understood what he meant—he also wasn't ready to leave Jessica. My guts twisted in an interesting new way. It was a different type of jealousy. The real, romantic kind. Magnify what I'd felt when Ryan had posted the pic in Louisville by about ten thousand.

"I can drive," I said.

He shot me a look. And, okay, stereotypical as it was, I was not a good driver. It had nothing to do with me being Asian. It had everything to do with the fact that I just didn't pay enough attention to the road. I'd get lost in thought and speed or miss stop signs. So I didn't drive unless I absolutely had to. And that wasn't often since I didn't have my own car.

"Well, what do you suggest?" I asked. "We can't stay on campus now and you can't drive."

He paused for a minute, and I was glad as I was still struggling to catch my breath. I really needed to do more cardio; I had no excuse for being so out of shape other than the fact that I hated cardio.

Eric rubbed his chin, even though I didn't see any options to mull over.

"Let's go sleep in the car," he said.

I couldn't have heard him correctly. "What?"

"Let's sleep in the car." He glanced at the time on his phone then put it away. "It'll be one o'clock by the time we get back to where we parked. If we sleep a few hours, we can take off at a decent time in the morning. Maybe look around one last time."

I couldn't argue with the fact that I was tired and my feet were now hurting. My gilded sandals were not made for track sprints. Plus, we really didn't have many options without driving, and it was appealing to have one more shot at finding Bri. Maybe my luck would change the next day. Selfishly, I wanted Eric's luck to stay the same.

Still, sleeping in the car next to him sounded like a disaster waiting to happen as we'd already kissed, I was pretty certain I snored, and we were staying so he could try to get his ex back.

But, really, what was one more calamity?

"All right," I said.

He blinked twice at me, then he nodded, and we started our long walk back to the car, passing by darkened buildings and towering trees.

"Thanks, by the way," Eric said.

"For what?" I tilted my head.

"Well, for not getting me arrested," he said.

"Oh, sure. Anything for you." I smiled brightly and batted my eyes.

"Impossible," he muttered.

And, yes, I knew that, but at least we were back to our normal jabs and I could almost ignore the fact that a flame lit up inside me just because I was near him.

CHAPTER THIRTY-SIX

Pro tip: if you want space from someone, trying to fall asleep next to him in a BMW 3 Series is not a good choice.

We made it back to Eric's car, reclined the seats, and kicked off our shoes. It felt so good to lie down barefoot that I almost considered sleeping in the car a good idea, but the likelihood I'd fall asleep was zero. I'd never camped out in a car, and way too much had happened that day. I tossed in various directions and couldn't get comfortable.

"You're a noisy bedmate," Eric said.

"Don't make this worse," I replied, without opening my eyes.

"You sound wide awake," he said.

"So do you."

"I am."

I glanced over at him. It was mostly dark in the car, but we were parked beneath the orangey glow of a streetlight, and I could see he was looking at me.

"Why do people drink? This is terrible," Eric said. "I can feel my heartbeat in my throat."

"You are a lightweight, a control freak, and a terrible drunk," I said. "Not everyone is."

"I'm not drunk anymore. I'm just tired and I can already feel a headache coming on."

"Wait." I grabbed my purse, dug around, and gave him the little travel container of Advil I took everywhere.

"Lifesaver," he said. "Can I have some of your water?"

The bottle I'd bought at the rest stop was still in the cup holder.

"Have at it," I said.

"Thank you." He sat up, opened my water, and guzzled some. "I'll get you another later."

"Good. I don't want your germs."

He shot me a look, and I wanted to shrivel and die because, yes, we'd definitely exchanged germs already. It was like I could feel my own chest caving in from the embarrassment of stumbling into that one.

Eric reclined again. "Do you want to talk about why you ran away?"

"Nope. Not a drop. Not even half a drop, thanks."

"I think we should—"

I shook my head. "No, Eric. We shouldn't."

"Oh, good. Maybe in four to five more years we can sort out tonight's misunderstanding."

All right, sometimes he could be a little funny.

We rested in the dark and I tried to clear my mind.

"Because if I—" he began. And I knew: he was going to keep going with this until I put a hard stop to it.

"Eric, look, it never happened, okay?" I said. "We never have to talk about it. I'll never want to talk about it. Let's just forget it—this entire trip never happened."

He was silent for a second. I was a little worried I'd hurt him as the silence dragged on.

"But we're still on the trip, so where does that fit into the secrecy paradigm?" he asked.

"Stop it. I'm sleeping," I said. But we could see each other's eyes even in the dark, and I could see his smile, which meant he probably could see mine.

"I've liked talking to you on this trip," he said. "I haven't been able to really talk to anyone in a long time."

"Is Jessica not the perfect confidante?" I said.

Yeah, bitter, party of one, your table is ready.

"No, definitely not. She . . . no, I couldn't talk to her about anything really."

I raised my head a little. "Eric, what do you like about her other than that she's hot?"

He paused, taking time to think about it. "I guess I liked having her attention and how special she made me feel. That out of all the guys at camp, she saw something in me. And yes, she's attractive, but she goes to UPenn so she's smart as well."

I was very sorry I asked. Now he was lying next to me, thinking about her.

"I liked going out with her, but I felt like I was filling a role in her life." He stared up at the car ceiling. "I checked the right boxes. And she did for me, too. I honestly wasn't fixated on her until she stopped talking to me. Then it became this mystery I had to solve, this game to win that I couldn't let go of—because I always play to win. Even when there's no point to it, even when the score is so lopsided, I can't make up the difference. I've had time to think about it on the drive down and all day today. There's something wrong with not missing the person but wanting her back."

"It's wrong?" I asked.

"Yeah, if it's about winning rather than wanting to be with her, it's definitely not right."

Now it was my turn to stare up at the ceiling.

"Am I like that with Bri?" I said, thinking aloud.

"Only you know, but I don't think so."

I lay there and thought about it. Truth was, I missed everything about Bri. I missed being able to hear her voice and share our inside jokes. I missed how she really listened to me and cared. I missed her stories and knowing what was happening in her world. I was dying to tell her about the whole UPenn debacle and to get her reactions—where she'd agree and where she'd disagree with my takes. I missed the person I could trust with anything. I just missed my friend.

"No, I don't think so, either," I said.

"What I've been going over and over again in my head is that even if Jessica does contact me, it'll be because she's jealous. Because she doesn't want me to move on with someone else. And not wanting someone else to have you isn't the same as someone wanting to be with you. Too many guys I know get confused, but they're not the same."

Apparently Eric had deep thoughts after he drank.

"And here I thought we'd be pulling a *Say Anything* tomorrow," I said.

He knit his eyebrows. "Huh?"

"The movie, *Say Anything.*"

Same puzzled expression.

"Ugh, Eric. It's a classic. I know I've watched way too many movies because of my dad, but it's the one where the guy holds up the boom box under the girl's window to try to get her back."

"What's a boom box?" Eric asked.

I leaned my face into the leather. "If I had a pillow, I'd smother you with it."

He laughed. "I'm kidding. I know what a boom box is."

I turned on my side, facing him.

"It was his grand gesture," I said. "And it's become iconic."

"I know what you're referring to," he said. "Well, I didn't know the movie title, but I've heard of the scene. You'd be fun to watch a movie with."

I shook my head. "No, I'm not."

"Do you talk during the movie?" Eric asked.

"What? Of course not."

"Then you're not intolerable. Jessica and I went to a movie

once, and she scrolled on her phone and answered messages most of the time."

She continued to sound awesome.

"I meant I'm intolerable about dissecting it afterward," I said. "My dad has taught me way too much craft."

Teagan and Bri would listen to me for a little while post movie, and then they limited my rants to a Five-Minute Miller Analysis. Otherwise, I'd go on and on as my brain picked apart scenes, and really, no one other than my dad wanted to talk about it that much. They were more interested in saying they liked it or that it was scary rather than looking at why they felt that way. They didn't want to analyze what the screenwriter did to elicit those feelings, and yeah, I got it. Sometimes I bored myself.

"That's why I think you'd be fun," Eric said, yawning.

His yawn triggered mine, and I'd finally found a comfortable spot, curled on my side with my hands as a sort of pillow. Miraculously, sleep was pulling me under.

"I assure you, I'm not," I said. "Good night, Eric."

"Good night, Kelsie."

Thirty seconds later he was out cold. And while I was almost asleep, I now was jealous of his superhuman ability to pass out. And how handsome he looked when he slept. And how I really wanted to kiss him again even though this was all doomed.

"I ran away because I'm so into you," I whispered. "And I wanted this to be real instead of your distraction from someone else."

Then I closed my eyes and fell asleep too.

CHAPTER THIRTY-SEVEN

The sun woke me up, which was . . . unexpected. I figured at most I'd get, like, two or three hours of sleep in the car, but as I became more awake, I realized it was well after sunrise. I stretched and looked over at the driver's seat, expecting to find Eric asleep next to me. Instead, he was sitting up behind the wheel and there was coffee in the cup holders.

Apparently I'd slept through a whole Dunkin' run.

The clock said 8:05 a.m. It was almost time to head back to Saratoga, and oh God, I'd forgotten to text my mother before we fell asleep.

Oh no.

I shot up, grabbed my purse, and rummaged for my phone. Sure enough, I had two texts and four missed calls from my mother.

Shit.

"Good morning?" Eric said.

"Hey, just a second, my mother is going drive down here to kill me," I said.

Now wide frigging awake, I pressed the green button to call her back. Mom picked up on the first ring. I was a dead woman.

"Kelsie," she said. "I've been so worried."

"Relax, Mom. I'm okay. I fell asleep at, like, midnight and forgot to text, but I'm just fine. I'm up, alive, and we're going to get breakfast soon."

I was careful to stay close to the truth as I couldn't lie, even by phone. I pulled down the visor and checked my raccoon eyes in the mirror. Making a face, I grabbed a napkin from Eric and wiped off the excess.

"Kel, this is not okay," she said.

I sighed and flipped the visor back. "I know. I didn't mean to worry you. I'm sorry. You must've been waiting up for me to text, and it was inconsiderate of me."

I paused, and there was dead silence on the other end.

"Hello?" I looked at the screen, which said I was still connected. I put the phone back to my ear.

"Who is this?" Mom said.

I looked around. "Um, your daughter?"

"No, you actually apologized," she said. "I didn't have to spend an hour dragging a half-assed 'sorry' out of you; therefore, you couldn't be my beloved child."

"Language," I said.

"Beloved daughter," Mom said.

I laughed. It was never too early to be roasted by your parent.

Then it dawned on me what she was saying. Did I have a problem apologizing? I didn't think so. I just didn't need to apologize much because apologizing meant you were wrong and I wasn't wrong that often, and okay, yeah, apparently I had a huge problem apologizing.

Add that to the ever-growing therapy list.

"Either way, I am sorry, Mom," I said. "I'll grovel when I get back, but I need to go. We'll be on the road soon. I love you."

She said goodbye, and I couldn't hang up fast enough because I had a ton of messages I needed to look at.

"Everything okay?" Eric asked. "You seem . . . caffeinated."

"Yeah, no, I don't know. Just give me a second, please. And thank you for the coffee." I pointed to the cup holder.

I started searching my email.

"I got a couple of doughnuts, bagels, and muffins, too." He gestured to a bag. "I've seen you bring in all three, so I wasn't sure what you'd be in the mood for."

"That's amazing, but I'd love a stick of gum first if you have any." I ran my tongue over my teeth. "I taste like a swamp."

"You're a charming ogre."

He handed me a piece of Orbit, and I chewed so hard, my jaw hurt as I went through all my texts and Instagram comments to Bri. The only distraction was Eric looking over at me every two seconds.

"Seriously, what are you intensely researching over there?" Eric asked. "Maybe I can help."

"I don't think you can," I murmured.

I used the search key in emails and not a one, nothing I sent to Bri included the word "sorry." The closest I'd come was telling her I shouldn't have said those things at her party. That was only yesterday, over a month after she'd stopped speaking to me. And it was still not an apology.

I closed my eyes for a long blink. I'd never apologized to my best friend.

Sighing, I pinched the bridge of my nose. God, I was such a dick. I really was Edison electrocuting pets and racing to the patent office.

"What is it?" Eric said.

I rubbed my face. "I'm an asshole."

"Hmm, why this time?"

I paused for long enough to scrunch my nose at him. "I've never apologized to Bri."

"Really? Never?" he asked. Somehow he managed to not sound judgmental, just confused.

"Yeah."

"Yikes, wow, you really are an asshole." He smiled a little.

"Yeah, thanks. I don't know why I didn't. I guess . . . I hate admitting that I'm wrong. But I wasn't even aware I had this problem until now. Like . . . just now."

It had to be, at least in part, a Carver thing. We were used to always being right. Even kids caught cheating had valid excuses and felt justified because of the pressure. But then I thought about Eric. While he'd never apologized for beating the crap out of the middle school bullies, he'd apologized for pushing me off the balance beam and for laughing during my speech. Just like that. No issues about it. No couched terms. He said he was sorry, even when he didn't remember doing anything wrong.

"Why is it so easy for you to apologize?" I asked. "You can't possibly enjoy admitting you made a mistake."

I rooted around in the Dunkin' bag and tore off a chunk of sesame bagel with cream cheese. I then passed the bag over to him.

"It's not easy. Or it wasn't," Eric said. "I don't remember apologizing when Jay was alive. School even suspended me because I wouldn't fake an apology. And I wouldn't tell people what I liked about them either—compliments, things like that. They were thoughts that entered my head, but for some reason I wouldn't say them out loud. But after he died . . . there was so much I'd wanted to say. So much I hadn't, and I didn't want that to happen again."

I nodded and spit out my gum, gently depositing it in a napkin in the trash bag. Then I drank some coffee and ate the bagel, picking crumbs off my lap, while he somehow managed to eat a muffin without a single speck going astray.

"Makes sense," I said. I needed to get better at both of those. I'd lost Bri and there was so much I still needed to tell her. "I hope we can find Bri this morning."

"I hope so, too," Eric said. "Where should we look?"

I was about to answer, but his phone chimed with a specific tone. He reached his hand out, but didn't check it. Instead, he stared at his cell like he was uncertain.

Putting two and two together, I realized who it was. Then it felt like the bagel had turned to lead in my stomach. I swallowed hard.

"It's, um, it's Jessica, isn't it?" I asked.

"Yeah." He rubbed the back of his neck. I could tell he wanted to look at the message, but for some reason he wasn't reading it.

"You know what would solve this mystery?" I pointed to his phone.

And yes, it hurt. It did. But the reality was this was why we'd taken the trip. Yes, he'd drunkenly kissed me and he'd seemed kinda over her before we fell asleep, but now he was sober and it was clear he still missed her. He lit up when he'd heard that text chime. Like Pavlov's dog, ears perked and ready to go. Maybe one day a boy would light up like that over me. But for now, he wasn't the one. And I'd learned my lesson about standing in the way of someone when they really wanted something. Plus, what was one more entry into my log of failure? I could at least try to be the supportive friend to Eric I should've been to Bri. Because I wanted the people I loved to be happy.

And oh God, did I love him? Was that love—wanting him to be happy even if it wasn't with me?

Wow, it sucked.

Eric picked up his phone and read the screen, then he put it back into the cup holder. He tugged at his ear and pursed his lips.

"Well?" I held my breath. Hopefully it would be like removing a Band-Aid—a world of hurt but over with quickly.

"She said she just got my flowers. She was studying all night in her room."

It seemed believable at first. Maybe she'd already had dinner when we stopped by and maybe she had noise-canceling headphones on and hadn't heard him knock. But there hadn't been a sound. Like true stalkers, we'd listened at her door. Then I remembered she was in a normal dorm room—those didn't have bathrooms inside.

"She didn't need to use the bathroom, or go brush her teeth?" I arched my eyebrow.

"It's what she said." He shrugged.

"Oh." It was obviously a lie, but if it was one he wanted to believe, I wouldn't convince him otherwise.

I stayed quiet.

He folded the bakery bag back up. "I'm . . . I'm going to go talk to her. You can—"

"I'll come with you," I said.

He shot me a look.

"I mean to use the bathroom," I added. Because once again I had to pee. "And to maybe see Bri. Not to be a third wheel."

"Oh, yeah," he said. "Maybe we can stop at admissions on the way so I can wash my face too."

Spectacular. He'd look even better going to see her.

I nodded, even though another hole had opened in my heart. But, all the same, we got out of the car and headed back to the UPenn campus together for the last time.

CHAPTER THIRTY-EIGHT

The admissions building was open and they were nice enough to let us use the restrooms. I stared in the mirror after washing off my face. I wasn't in bad shape considering I'd been wearing the same clothes for twenty-four hours. Also, I had a little disposable toothbrush in my bag, likely thanks to my mom, so I got to brush my teeth. I combed my hair and reapplied my makeup. Everything else would have to wait until I got home.

I finished fixing myself and sighed in the mirror, staring at my reflection. I was stalling.

Ugh. I was still a bad person.

I forced my legs to walk, which turned into me shuffle-stomping out of the building. Trying to be a better person was really hard.

I met Eric out front on the stone steps and he smiled at me. The whole thing would've been easier if he didn't look at me like I was the only girl in the world.

I didn't know where to go, so I found myself walking with him to Jessica's building. I was consumed with thoughts of Eric, and he was probably consumed with thoughts of her, and I was in the worst spot in this little love triangle—or love . . . angle.

"I'll just wait outside," I said. I wasn't even sure why I was still with him, except that's how we'd been since we arrived at the campus—a unit.

Her building loomed in the distance. She'd want to officially date him again and that would be it for whatever road-trip connection we'd formed. Then he and I would act like we barely knew each other in the halls of Carver.

Super-great senior year incoming.

"Hmm? Oh, yeah, okay," he said.

He'd already started forgetting about me even though I was still next to him.

Eric looked unfairly handsome as we hadn't showered. He even had a glow to him. I threw on my red sunglasses.

"Those look good on you," he said.

"Um, thanks," I said.

More quiet.

We walked up to her dorm and lingered at the bottom of the ramp. I was waiting for him to go up, but he seemed to be trying to say something to me. He opened his mouth and closed it a couple of times while shifting his weight from foot to foot.

I waited, but he didn't get the chance to say anything

because the door opened and there was Jessica. All five-eleven of her came out of Hill College House wearing a tiny purple tank and jeans.

She was somehow taller than I'd imagined, even though all her measurements were posted online for some modeling reason. Her face wasn't as flawless as it was on Instagram, but that's what filters were for, and let's be honest, she was still beautiful.

Jessica was typing something into her phone, but she was bound to notice Eric once she looked up, so I did the adult thing and ducked behind a nearby tree. I leaned against the bark and held my breath.

Don't judge. What the hell else was I supposed to do?

It dawned on me that I looked ridiculous cowering behind a tree, so I changed my posture to casually leaning against it. I took out my phone so it wouldn't seem like I was eavesdropping on their conversation.

Note: I was completely eavesdropping. Moral high ground would have to wait.

"Eric," Jessica said. "Oh my God. You're here?"

"Hi, Jess," he said.

She laughed at nothing. "Thank you again for all the flowers. They were too sweet."

"You're welcome."

They were either silent or whispering or making out. I really hoped they weren't making out.

"But I don't understand; why did you come to UPenn?" she asked.

"To tour the campus," he replied. "But also . . . I guess I'd wanted to know what had happened. If I'd done something wrong. And if you were okay."

"Oh, Eric. I really had a good summer with you, I did, but you're in high school in New York and I'm here. I know you've messaged, but I've just been so busy with starting college and everything that I forgot to write back. But no, you didn't do anything wrong at all."

Oh, come on—busy? How long would it have taken to respond to a text? She had time to party with her girlfriends but not two seconds to press a reaction on one of his messages?

"I . . ." He trailed off. If there was a merciful God, he was not whispering in her ear. "You know, it's funny, I had all these things I wanted to say before I came down and even when I left you the flowers, but now . . . I guess I'm glad you're doing well and that there aren't hard feelings."

"That's really sweet," she said.

Yes, she'd used the same expression twice.

"You're such a good guy, Eric," she added. "My life has just been a blur with studying, and yoga, and photo shoots, and trying to keep up with DMs."

Ah, yes, life blurring . . . yoga.

"But I don't know . . . maybe when things slow down we'll find each other again," she said.

"What do you mean?" he asked.

"I mean, who knows what will be," she said. "Only the moon and the stars see at night."

I cringed. She was a walking frigging Instagram post. I stopped myself from groaning . . . just barely. How could Eric like this girl? How could I like a guy who liked this girl?

"Yeah, I guess," he said. "Well, I should get going. You probably have to head to class."

There was silence for a few seconds. He must've been walking away. I could hear sandals on the pavement coming my way.

"Wait . . . that's it?" she asked.

I couldn't see him shrug so much as I could feel it.

"Yeah," he said. "It's like you said—you have your life here and I have mine in New York."

"And a new girl . . ."

Oh. So she was exactly the jealous type.

Eric uttered some kind of "eh" noise. "Something like that."

"But she isn't me, is she?"

I swear I stopped breathing. My face went cold. Of course the second he'd stopped chasing after her, she wanted him back. It was all too predictable. And he was going to tell her that I wasn't her. Her voice was laced with sex. Sex never laced anything of mine. The truth was, Jessica was a tall, wannabe Victoria's Secret model and I was an oddball little sidekick.

Was there even a choice to be made?

I swayed in the rhythm of my heartbeat while waiting for him to put the final nail in the coffin of our road-trip chemistry.

"She very much isn't you and I like that," he said. "Take care, Jess."

I heard her make some scoffing noise but more important, heard his sandals coming quickly toward me. I struggled to seem like I hadn't heard a thing, but I wasn't sure what that would even look like.

He came around the tree, and I think it's safe to say I failed abysmally. We stared at each other for a second.

I pursed my lips, trying to formulate a sentence, and he ran his hand over his hair.

"Are you . . . are you okay?" I asked.

"Yeah," he nodded. "Yeah."

We took turns nodding. If two aliens were trying to play at being casual humans, they'd look like me and Eric standing to the side of the Hill College House dorm.

He'd just put an end to things with Jessica. And while I was proud of him, I was also stunned. That hadn't been what we came here to do, and Eric didn't know how to veer from his goals. I was certain he had mixed feelings about it. But I did know he deserved more than being a maybe in the future. And yes, okay, I was glad that he was fully single.

It was already starting to get warm, which meant it was getting later. People passed by to go to breakfast and classes. I wondered if Bri would visit the campus today or be on her way back to Seattle whenever she woke up. She still hadn't posted since the dinner shot or replied to the dozens of comments. And now that things were resolved with Jessica, it only highlighted how unsuccessful I'd been with Bri. And how little time we had left.

I didn't want to rush Eric, particularly as he had that far-off nebula stare, but I didn't have much of a choice.

"Should we . . . should we try one more time to find Bri?" I asked. "I don't know if she's awake yet, but I mean, it's not like we can stay forever."

He returned to our solar system. "Yeah. Are you thinking of staking out the hotel again?"

"It's as good a guess as any," I said.

I searched his face, trying to figure out if he needed more time. "Are you sure you're good?"

"Yes, it's just . . . a lot," he said.

No kidding.

CHAPTER THIRTY-NINE

We traced the now familiar path from the heart of the campus to the Inn at Penn. I kept glancing over at Eric, but he stared straight ahead.

I was glad for my shades; I could stay hidden behind them. I'd been as surprised as Jessica when he'd said he liked how I wasn't her. Did that mean that he like-liked me?

Ugh, why did it feel like I was twelve? Although, honestly, there were twelve-year-olds with more romantic experience than me. Hanna, the little crimson goblin, had already had a "boyfriend," and she was going into third grade.

The more I thought about it, though, the less realistic it was that Eric had been for real. It must've all been a ruse. Just like posting the selfies of him and me to spark Jessica's jealousy. He probably said that to get back at her for leaving him dangling for days. For wanting to keep him on the back burner with some moon and stars bullshit. It was understandable if he'd said it to upset her, to take her ego down a notch. I wasn't supposed to have heard him anyhow.

I was caught in a kind of no-man's-land—admit I'd eavesdropped and ask what he meant (not appealing) or pretend I hadn't heard. I chose the latter. Still, the silence was getting to me.

"A Kool-Aid for your thoughts," I said.

He smiled slowly. "Lots on my mind. Sorry, I don't mean to be a lousy stalking partner."

"No worries, friend," I said.

Maybe if I started calling him friend or buddy or pal now, it would hurt less when he told me he wanted to be friends later. I was pretty short on friends anyhow, so it might've been a good idea to have Eric.

"What are you going to do if we can't find Bri?" he asked. "I'd stay longer, but I really can't miss tonight's game or the warm-ups."

"It's okay. I don't want to stay. I guess if we can't find her, I'll send her one last email apologizing and then I'll have to let it go. It's funny, I'm okay with it. This whole time I was so focused on searching for answers that I didn't see the facts right in front of me. But now I see it and . . . at least I understand."

"I know how that feels," Eric said.

I wondered if he saw Jessica for what she truly was.

He pressed the crosswalk button, and we walked over to the Inn at Penn.

Eric held the door open to the hotel, and I searched the sitting area where we'd crashed the night before. Unfortunately, there was just an elderly man reading the paper. I wasn't lucky enough for Bri to happen to be in the lobby.

I peered into the restaurant, which was pretty busy for a Friday morning. I scanned every table, standing on my tiptoes to see all the customers, and there she was. I passed her while scanning and had to stop and go back because it wasn't just a blonde with wavy hair—she wore it straight today. It wasn't a doppelgänger or a phantom text vibration. It was Bri sitting at breakfast with her mother.

Or, her mother was on her phone outside and Bri was sitting across from an empty chair and her mother's laptop.

I blinked to lose the mirage, but it persisted. It was Brianna and yet I still couldn't believe my eyes. Had my luck really changed so dramatically? I wanted to go to her, but my feet froze to the ground, unwilling to move.

"Wow, there she is," Eric said, coming up behind me. Distractingly close, if I'm being honest.

"I . . . I know," I said.

"What's wrong?" he asked.

"I just . . . How can I go up to her after everything? I don't know if . . . maybe an email would be better. Maybe she doesn't want to hear from me. Maybe we should just leave."

Suddenly, ambushing her seemed like a terrible idea.

"She's your best friend, Kelsie," Eric said.

"I don't . . . I don't know what to tell her."

He shook his head. "You know what to say. You already told me."

"What if she doesn't want to hear it?" I turned to face him.

His expression softened, probably from the utter panic in my eyes. "Then you're in the same spot, really. But you have a chance to set things right. It may not work, but you owe it to you and Bri to try. And most of all: she deserves to hear you apologize even if she rejects it. You don't know what I'd give to have the same chance."

I grimaced. What could I really say to that? Sorry you didn't get to apologize to your dead best friend, but I'm not doing this even though mine is only a few yards away?

Thus, completely ashamed of my cowardice, I took a deep breath, then a step, then another, then another, until I was next to Bri. She deserved to publicly order me out of the restaurant if she wanted to.

"Hey," I said.

Bri startled in her chair. "Oh my God! Kel?"

She blinked hard then smiled brightly, like there was nothing wrong. I couldn't help but smile back. Maybe this would be easier, better than I'd ever thought.

"Are you really here?" she asked.

Okay, deep breath. "I am."

She shook her head a little, her blond hair waving. "Wow. This is . . . surreal."

"It is a fantastically long story, but I came down here to try to find you," I said.

Her forehead wrinkled. "Um . . . okay."

"We haven't talked since you left, and you haven't . . ."

She frowned, staring down at the tablecloth. Right. She didn't want to talk about this. But at least she hadn't ordered me to leave yet.

Somehow, I put air in my lungs and a resolution in my head and said, "I just wanted to tell you in person that I'm sorry. I'm really sorry I said those things at your party. I'm sorry I couldn't have been happier and more supportive, like I should've been. But I thought I'd lose you and I didn't know how to be myself without you. But that's my issue. I'm sorry for not being a better friend, for not seeing what you needed. I'm sorry for judging your relationship with your mom. I'm just . . . sorry."

Bri stared straight ahead, and I stood there feeling like crumpled aluminum foil—used up but still somehow whole. I'd at least apologized, and even if she couldn't forgive me, I'd tried.

"Hey, I couldn't get off the phone and—"

I turned and Elaine Taylor was back at the table. She was as pretty as I remembered. Her blond hair was shoulder length and dyed so it was closer to Bri's shade. Elaine had a full face of makeup on, highlighting her hazel eyes, and she wore a silk shell and casually chic jeans. She probably loved when she was mistaken for Bri's sister instead of mother.

Elaine looked at me with a puzzled expression for a second, then recognition lit her face. "Kelsie? Kelsie Miller?"

I nodded.

"Wow, hello. It's been a long time," Elaine said. "You've changed so much! You look so beautiful!" She came over and gave me a limp hug.

It sounded like a compliment, but, like . . . was I not pretty three years ago? I guessed not.

"It's been a while, Ms. Taylor," I said.

Elaine tilted her head. "You know it's Elaine. Feel free to join us for breakfast. We still have an hour before we have to head to the airport." She'd obviously not looked at her daughter once. Bri was pale and staring blankly forward.

"No, that's okay. I . . . I'm here with someone and I don't want to interrupt," I said.

"Who are you here with?" Bri asked. It was like she'd woken from a stupor, but she spoke in a low voice.

"Um . . . well . . . Eric Mulvaney Ortiz," I said. "I'd texted you. . . ."

Her brown eyes got wide as saucers and she looked up at me. I did a little mime trying to convey that being with him was part of the very long story. Bri nodded once, just getting me the way she used to. It filled me with a warmth that quickly evaporated, leaving me that much colder for it being gone.

"My phone has barely worked since I dropped it in the sink at dinner," she said.

Well, that explained the lack of posting.

"Oh, I love Eric," Elaine said with a smile. Of course she did, didn't we all? "He's more than welcome to join us too!"

"That's really kind of you, but we actually have to be going,"

I said, looking over at him. He was studying the bar offerings, probably wondering if they all tasted like Kool-Aid. "He has a game later today in New York."

"Oh, okay. Another time then," Elaine said.

It was a pleasant, meaningless Elaine thing to say. Really, what other time were we going to happen to run into each other when she lived in Seattle?

Her phone went off. "Ugh, excuse me. I have to take this. It was good to see you, Kelsie. And say hi to your parents for me."

"I will," I said.

"Don't wait for me to order, Bri. Accounting just cannot seem to get this project done, so I don't know how long this will take. Order something I'd like too, please."

"Okay, Mom," Bri said.

I got the feeling this happened a lot—that Bri was left sitting alone at a nice table in a fancy restaurant while her mother worked.

Elaine smiled over her shoulder at me then walked away.

We both watched her mom go. I thought I'd be more hostile to seeing Elaine again, but I wasn't. She was exactly as I remembered, but she was still Bri's mom. And, really, she was trying. It wasn't her fault that I didn't think it was enough.

"Anyhow, I'll leave you alone," I said. "I'm sorry I surprised you, but I wanted to say it all in person. And to see you again. I hope you get into UPenn. Really, I hope you get everything you want. And just . . . thank you for all those years."

With that, I turned and walked back toward Eric. He stood

watching me, his eyes continually scanning my face. I wanted to dissolve into him, but we didn't have that kind of relationship. Who knew what it was other than the start of a friendship, but it was great to have that.

As I walked, I replayed my favorite memories with Bri: screaming and hiding together in playgrounds, singing musicals in her basement, sleepovers at my house, and thinking we were so cool in middle school as we sneaked cigarettes and hung out on her dock with our bare feet skimming the water. We'd been so happy to both get into Carver and to keep attending the same school. We'd done homework and projects together in Teagan's bakery and thrown cookies at each other when the other accidentally fell asleep. We'd painted each other's nails, sitting in her ridiculously large bathroom with sheet masks on and leave-in conditioner in our hair. I'd made her a sparkly two-sided sign when she'd taken her driver's test and waited at her dad's house for her to get back. One side congratulated her, the other, in case she failed, said at least she gave the instructor hell. And there was the last day of junior year, the last moment where we were normal in the hall, talking about the summer. The one right before her mother texted her, offering to have her live in Seattle.

Now that part of my life was over. I wasn't sure what lay ahead of me, but I did know it would never be the same. Maybe that was okay. Or maybe it wasn't, but it was happening either way.

I stopped in front of Eric. "I told her."

He nodded although he looked behind me, back at Bri.

"Come on." I headed toward the door.

It was enough.

It was enough to have gotten to see her and had the chance to tell her I was sorry in person.

It was time for us to go.

CHAPTER FORTY

As we went outside, storm clouds rolled in like they could sense my feelings. I looked up at the heavy sky, the weight of the past month pressing me into the earth. Eric's hand grazed my lower back.

"Hey, it's okay," he said.

We were two steps beyond the door and I took one more before hanging my head.

"I don't know that it is," I said.

"It will be. I promise it will."

I took a deep breath and looked him in the eye. "What if it's not?"

He started to reply but stopped, staring past me. I turned and saw Bri jogging toward us.

She stopped a few feet away and shot Eric the most confused look she possessed, then she faced me.

"You said you were sorry?" she asked.

"Yes," I said. "Apparently I have quite an issue with that."

She glanced to the side. Okay, so I had a major issue and needed to reevaluate myself if the people who'd known me the longest all knew this except for me.

"But I am sorry, Bri. I was way too judgmental and it was messed up for me to say those things at your party. And then to not apologize—" I looped my thumbs in my back pockets.

"I was waiting for an apology, honestly, but then . . ." she began.

"I know. I never did—until now. I owed you more. I owed our friendship more."

"You did," she said. "You owed us more. As time went on, the more messages you sent that didn't include an apology, the angrier I got at you for not saying you were sorry. But I should've replied to you. You were trying, and I could've said why I was angry. Sometimes I felt like you should know everything that was going through my mind because you usually did, but I'm sorry too."

I shook my head. "You have nothing to apologize for."

"No, I do. I knew you were just trying to protect me."

"Instead, I hurt you," I said.

She pursed her lips. "And instead, I lashed out at you because you voiced the exact fear I was trying to ignore."

I shook my head again. "I was out of line. She does want you—she always has. I just couldn't understand her being different from my mom and dad."

She shrugged. "You were right in a way—about her. But I've

always . . ." She paused then shoved her hands in the pockets of her romper. "I always thought I could have this incredible relationship with my mom, like how you are with yours, if I just tried harder, or if we started over, or if we were away from my dad and her hostility toward him. And I . . . I couldn't handle anyone telling me the truth when I'd made the decision and I wanted so badly to believe in her. I love her, but she has . . . limitations."

Bri was so much more insightful and understanding than I'd given her credit for. I hadn't had enough faith in her to see her mom. She did understand who Elaine was, completely. I was the one who hadn't seen the full picture. I'd been so focused on losing her that I'd lost sight of what my best friend was dealing with.

"Anyhow, I'm glad I sat next to you in kindergarten," Bri said. "I've always been glad I hopped into that seat."

If joy could've exploded through my chest, it would've. Instead, tears burst from my eyes.

"I love you, Bri," I said, sniffling.

"I love you too," she said.

I opened my arms and she opened hers and we fell into each other. She leaned down to put her chin on my shoulder. I was, incidentally, an ugly crier.

"I'm really, really sorry," I whispered.

"I know you are," she said. "I am too."

"I've missed you so much."

"I've missed you, too."

We hugged until she lifted her head, leaving my shirt damp with tears. I wiped at the makeup that was surely running down my face and she did the same, fanning her long lashes. She pulled herself together, then looked over at Eric and back at me. She stuck out her hand like, okay, tell me.

"It's part of the fantastically long story I mentioned," I said. Because how in the world was I supposed to get into it while standing on the sidewalk?

She smiled. "I'd love to hear it."

"So I'll . . . I'll text you, then?" I said.

She nodded and smiled her slightly crooked grin. "Yeah. I'll get my phone fixed when I land and I'll talk to you later. Good to see you, Eric."

"You too, Bri," he said.

She trotted back into the restaurant, and for the first time in a while, I felt good. Really good.

I looked over at Eric and he had the goofiest grin on his face. "Oh my God, you're such a loser," I said.

He shrugged with a boyish smile.

I rolled my eyes and nudged my shoulder into his arm. The same way I had before we kissed; sure enough, the goddamn flame lit up again.

"I'm really happy for you, Kel," he said.

"I know you are. Thank you for all this, Eric. It means . . ." I choked up because apparently it was going to be a crying day. "It means the world to me."

"You're welcome. Thank you, too."

I knit my eyebrows at him. "For what?"

"For a lot of things, but most of all for showing me what I want," he said.

I really hoped he would apply to UPenn and play football and get to live his dreams. He deserved them.

"Let's go home," I said.

He put out his arm in the direction of the BMW. "Your chariot awaits."

"Thank you, kind sir."

I looked back at Bri, and UPenn, and all that Eric and I had gained and lost. Then we crossed the street and made our way to the car.

CHAPTER FORTY-ONE

Big, fat raindrops splashed against the windshield just as Eric started the engine. The timing was incredible. The timing of all of it really.

We listened to music and didn't talk much on the monotonous stretch of highway. So much had happened. There was still a lot to process, and I had a feeling I'd be thinking about parts of the trip for years to come. But one thing I knew: I wanted to do something for Eric. It had been his idea to go to UPenn. It was his badgering, but also him opening up and talking to me about how he viewed things that allowed me to see what I'd been missing. About him, yes, but also about me and Bri. He was a major reason why Bri had texted me from her iPad when she got on the restaurant Wi-Fi. Why we'd been able to pick up where we'd left off. It wasn't like nothing had happened between us, but it was the start of a new normal.

And yet the trip hadn't worked out for him. He'd said he

was fine and that he'd just wanted a concrete end to things with Jessica, but he'd still spent all that time and energy and had nothing to show for it. Except that the two of us weren't enemies anymore.

While my friendship was quite the prize, I doubted that was what he'd had in mind when planning to go to Pennsylvania.

He was on a hands-free call with his dads, and I pulled up the recruitment page for UPenn football. For all I knew, they already had Eric on their radar because of his football camp, but in case they didn't, I found the assistant coach's email and sent them the article about him being the Hero of Carver and told them more about how he was Dominican on Dr. Ortiz's side and Irish on his surrogate's. How he was on track to be valedictorian of Carver, a volunteer at the soup kitchen and elementary school, and just generally a good person.

The thing was, I didn't even need to lie or embellish. Eric was all those things.

He hadn't brought up the kiss, and I was glad. I was fine going to the grave without ever discussing it. I was in no mood for a strained conversation about how he'd been drunk and we'd be better off as friends who never mentioned it again. But I did have a question for him.

Okay, I had many questions for him, but this one in particular didn't involve me.

We were cruising up the Turnpike when I decided to bring it up. Bri had messaged that she'd been on the eleven o'clock tour yesterday. Her mother had booked it. It was like she didn't even know Bri. Then I thought about Eric's surrogate situation and how much we ever know our parents.

"Can I ask you something?" I said, turning toward him.

He lowered the radio volume. "Sure."

"I promise there's a sequitur in my head, but have you decided whether or not you'll talk to your surrogate?"

He breathed in, then looked over at me. "Not what I thought you were going to ask."

"What did you think I'd ask?" I said.

He looked at me out of the corner of his eye, and it was like his gaze speared my lower stomach. Honestly, I hadn't even been sure he remembered kissing me, but something in his glance told me he did.

A smirk lit his lips. "Can't think of anything."

Was he really going to be like this?

"Well, that's good." I shot him a look that said: Answer the question, Eric.

He rubbed his forehead. "I don't know. It seems like everything in my world has been turned upside down in the past twenty-four hours."

"I understand," I said. "It's a lot to process."

It probably wasn't the right time to discuss his situation. It might take Eric weeks or months or maybe even years to come to a decision on what he wanted to do. And it was wrong to push him.

"It is," he said. "But I know you get it more than anyone."

"I . . . I think so."

"What would you do?" he asked.

That was a good question. Bri was right when she said I had a great relationship with my mom. My dad, too, for that matter. What would I do if my birth mother had contacted me? If she'd not only wanted to get to know me but to also introduce me to a half-sibling out of nowhere?

"I guess I'd want to know why she'd contacted me after seventeen years. But maybe it's always the same: We're their children who they gave up as babies. They have a history with us, even if it's a short one; meanwhile, we don't remember them at all. On the one hand, I don't know if I'd want to open that door. I love my family just the way they are—even the red gremlin. On the other, what harm would it do? Knowing my biological mother or sibling wouldn't take away from what I have with my family. I spent too many years thinking new connections would dull the ones I had. But this is a hypothetical situation for me and a real one for you. You'll decide what's right, and it doesn't have to be the same answer. I don't think there's one correct answer."

He exhaled and nodded along. "Essay instead of multiple choice."

"Exactly."

He ran his hand over his hair. "I guess I have to think about whether I want to open myself up to this other world."

"I think it's fine if you don't. It was a lot to spring on you. We're supposed to make all these adult choices now, when we're not really adults. I mean, I'm not. You kinda are."

"Some of the time."

"Aside from Kool-Aid."

He smiled at me. "I'll have to give it more thought and talk to my dads about the whole thing. But you're right—knowing the surrogate wouldn't take away from what I have with my family."

It was a reasonable response. Typical, levelheaded Eric instead of the off-kilter Eric of the past week. The one who wanted to leap down to UPenn on a prayer and give up his medical career to play football. The one I came to really like.

A deep sadness hit me like a tidal wave. Would things just go back to the way they were, now? Even after everything we'd experienced? He'd return to being the hero of Carver and I'd keep battling him in all our classes, and then there'd be the one-off night in my memory that haunted me?

"I'm sure talking it over will help," I said.

I stared out the window for a while, not wanting to look at him. I didn't want to think about him saying he'd never let anyone hurt me or the way his lips felt on my wrist, which of course meant those two things were all I could think about. That, and I could feel him looking at the back of my head.

"Are you tired?" he asked.

I stretched my shoulders, and yes, my whole body was fatigued. "Kinda, yeah."

"Take a nap if you want," he said.

"You sure? I don't want you falling asleep without my scintillating discourse."

"I'll manage."

I turned to look at him, and he gave me a small smile.

"Are you sure? We really did have a long night," I said.

"Yeah, I have a lot to think through anyhow," he said.

Okay, so he didn't want to talk to me anymore. Got it, loud and clear.

I reclined the seat and tried to get comfortable. But it was hard to lie still when a deep and heavy pressure was crushing my heart.

When we'd started the trip, I thought that resolving things with Bri would fix everything wrong with my life, but instead I'd added a new complication. And he was sitting next to me.

CHAPTER FORTY-TWO

By the time I woke up, we were already in New York and we'd be back home in a little more than half an hour, according to the GPS.

I yawned and sat up, surprised I'd been out that long.

"Good morning," Eric said.

Technically, it was afternoon.

"Top of the morn'," I said.

At least waking up this time I could actually say good morning and not scramble to text my mom. I'd messaged her right as we'd left Philadelphia. She'd said we needed to talk when I got home (meaning I was still a dead woman) but to drive safe (maybe there'd be some mercy).

"Glad to see you didn't crash while I was asleep," I said. "Were you okay?"

He smiled. "Yeah, I was fine. I don't really need that much sleep—six hours and I'm good."

"How? Oh, wait . . . you're a morning person." I frowned at him.

"You know I am," he said.

I did know that. I knew his favorite ice cream was butter pecan, although he was allergic to pistachios. That his favorite color was orange. That he'd reorganize sandwiches so that everything was equally distributed and the bites would all be about the same. Our long connection had allowed me to feel an attraction to him like I'd never felt before. Turned out Bri was right: I was probably demisexual. It seemed super fun to have to know someone for nearly my whole life to feel attracted to them, but I'd read people could form an emotional bond within months instead of, say, twelve years. It might not always be this way for me.

At least I had to hope.

Still, realizing I was demi explained why I'd never felt attracted to anyone I met at a party or while hostessing. Labels could be a problem, but they could also help me understand. I didn't need to think there was something wrong with me or feel tempted to keep pushing myself to feel attracted to people I didn't know. It just would come in its own time.

Unfortunately for me, the attraction was present and accounted for.

"You look lost in thought," he said.

"That makes two of us." I cracked open a water he'd bought during his Dunkin' run that morning. True to his word, Eric had replaced the one he'd guzzled.

"A lot happened," he said.

"You can say that again," I said.

My phone chimed and it was Bri, messaging again from her iPad. She was in flight, but of course she had Wi-Fi, because she was in business class with her mom. She was harassing me for the full story, especially because she'd seen Eric's Instagram Story and finally got my text about kissing him.

It was official: every single person on earth had seen his Instagram. And now we had a mess to clean up.

"What do you want to tell people about your Instagram Story?" I asked.

He glanced over at me. "What do you mean?"

"I mean, everyone at Carver and their mother wants to know what's going on with us."

"It's not really anyone's business." He took a sip of his water.

I stared at him, but apparently that was all he had to say. "That's it?"

"Yeah. You don't agree?"

I blinked a few times. "I do, but . . . aren't you a teenage boy? How can you just leave it at that?"

He gave me a small smile. "I guess it's that I know people will say and think what they want. The truth never seems to matter. It happened when I got suspended, then after Jay died, and with almost every girl I've been seen with—even when we just happened to be sitting next to each other or at the store at the same time. It's too exhausting to care about that stuff. You and I know, and that's enough."

I still had some questions on that front, but I'd decided to save them for when I could process another emotion.

"I wish I could be as cool as you about all this," I said. "But I suppose you have experience. I haven't had a whole rumor mill after me."

"Of course you have. That's Carver's specialty," Eric said.

"No way." I hadn't dated anyone so there was nothing to tell. I'd been Teflon to gossip . . . until now. "What rumors have you heard?"

He raised his eyebrows at me.

"Okay, I did hear the one that I was gay," I said.

People thought maybe I was in the closet and that was why I hadn't dated anyone. Truly, the school could not accept that I was just uninterested. But the gay rumor came on the heels of my kissing a girl at a party, because I thought maybe they were right, so . . . fair enough. I hadn't figured that part out yet.

"And the one with Ryan Culligan . . ."

Well, there was a name from the past. I looked over at Eric. "Which one with Ryan Culligan? He moved when we were freshmen. . . ."

"Oh, that you were together. Whatever that's supposed to mean at fourteen. But people were certain of it."

"I'd never heard that one, but it wasn't far off," I said.

"Seriously?" Eric's voice rose at the end, and he actually turned toward me a bit.

You'd think from his wrinkled brow and stunned face that I'd whipped out a value pack of Mom-purchased condoms.

"I'd kind of liked him," I said.

"Ryan Culligan?" He made some noise that sounded like a scoff. Were we really doing this? The poor kid wasn't even there to defend himself.

"Does it matter?" I laughed. "You're being awfully serious about someone who lives in Louisville."

Was that jealousy I was picking up on? It couldn't be. Eric wasn't a jealous person, and Ryan had been gone for years. Also, to be jealous, Eric would've had to want me. And he didn't. Still, he was acting off.

"You know he's moving back, right?" Eric said.

I did not know that.

"You're kidding."

"Nope, he posted something about it," Eric said. "He'll be back around the second week of school. I guess Carver is allowing the transfer because he already attended."

Carver had become such a little sewing circle because generally they didn't allow transfers. We didn't have any new blood aside from freshmen. Technically, people could apply to transfer in from other magnet schools, but how often did someone move to the Saratoga area from another magnet that Carver felt was worthy? It hadn't happened in my time there.

Usually no one transferred out, either. It was too much of an opportunity to leave behind. We had unique classes like robotics and Japanese, and a ranking that was respected by every Ivy. Ryan was one of three people who'd left in the three years we'd attended. Bri being number three. The prospect of his return was yet another thing I couldn't process.

"What are you, Facebook friends with him or something?" I asked.

Eric shrugged. He really was friends with everyone.

It was shaping up to be an interesting senior year, though not at all in the way I'd planned.

"Ryan Culligan," he muttered.

"Careful, Eric, you sound jealous." I said "jealous" in a sing-song way.

Eric looked away from me. Apparently we were back to him not getting my jokes as we careened toward Saratoga and the way things used to be.

CHAPTER FORTY-THREE

Eric pulled into my driveway and unbuckled his seatbelt to stretch in the car. Mom must've taken the Subaru into work, which meant Dad was probably on a writing tear. Hanna had camp, so at least there'd be peace in the house until three o'clock. Unless Dad was trying to draft on his old-fashioned typewriter again (please, God, no).

I unbuckled and grabbed my purse, but I had no idea what to say to Eric. "I want . . . thank you."

"You're welcome. It was . . . I'm glad we went together," he said.

I nodded like a bobblehead. Something had felt off since he'd mentioned Ryan Culligan, and I wasn't sure how to fix it.

"Well, um . . . thanks again." I opened the car door and put a leg out.

"Kelsie," Eric said.

I turned back and looked at him. His lips parted and he

breathed heavily while staring at me. I waited. I could've waited forever, stuck in that moment. But he swallowed and looked away.

"See you around," he said.

"Yeah," I muttered.

I got out of the car and went up the front steps of our bungalow. I turned and Eric was still idling in the driveway. He had the old-school manners to wait until I was safely in the house, which took a little while. Unusually, the door was locked, and it took me a second to find my key. Finally, I located it, opened the door, then did a small wave because I was the worst.

He waved back and reversed out of my driveway. I went inside, shut the door, and pressed against it. I was sad to see him go. The spell was broken and we were back to our normal. But there was something about the way he'd said my name and the look on his face.

I was officially overthinking things. I took a deep breath and shook it off.

"Hello?" I called.

No one was home if the car was gone and the door was locked, but I figured I'd check.

I went all the way up to the attic, passing the murals I had painted. My parents always encouraged my art, even when it was on their walls.

I knocked on Dad's "studio door," but it was open and there was no answer. There was also no chaotic mess the way there normally was when he was working. Just his desk, chair, minifridge,

TV, and inspiration boards. Maybe today was an errand day. Dad often starred as the main character of our local Target.

With an empty house and feeling chiefly grimy, I showered. By the time I was dressed in blessedly clean clothes, I heard noises downstairs.

I hopped down the wooden stairs, and there were my dad and mom, which was strange since Mom should've been at work. Instead, they were giggling in the kitchen.

Were they high? I really could not deal with my parents taking up marijuana in their old age.

"Hey," I said.

"Oh, you're back, Kel!" Mom said.

This was not the reaction I'd expected. She was beaming. I'd thought I'd get a lecture until the sun went down, but instead she seemed happy to see me.

What the hell was this?

"What's . . . uh . . . what's going on?" I asked.

Dad came over and kissed the top of my still-wet head.

"You tell her, honey," Mom said.

I looked at my dad's smiling face. "Oh my God. Did you win?"

I could barely contain myself, standing on my tiptoes to hear the words fall from his lips. The ones that would change our lives forever.

"Oh, I didn't find out about that yet, Kel," Dad said.

I exhaled, crumpling inward. "I'm sorry, Dad. It's just that you both looked so excited."

Guilt hit me hard for even bringing it up. I knew it weighed on his mind, and it was cruel to poke him about it.

"Well, we are excited, though," Dad said.

"Why's that?" I asked.

He puffed out his chest. "You are looking at the newest screenwriter represented by Robert Quiñonez of International Screen LA."

"Holy shit! What?" I jumped into his arms and hugged him. "Oh my God, this is incredible. How? Tell me everything? Was this just from querying?"

Querying was, like, awful cover letters my dad had sent for years hoping to get an agency interested in representing him, but it was really difficult to land an agent. An agent could pitch his work directly to the big production companies, so agencies were very choosy. It was hard to sign with any in LA and even harder to get a good one that had a decent sales record. A great agency like ISLA was nearly impossible.

"Yes and no on querying," my dad said.

It was hard for me to focus on his words because he was beaming and I was so happy for him. It was amazing to see him so confident. His whole mood made me feel like I was floating. He'd been this close to quitting. He hated how he couldn't take us on the vacations or buy me a car when I got my license. Then on top of the financial strain, the rejections from far-off places were so difficult that he felt like he was being selfish even though we told him he wasn't. Project Light had seemed like the last competition he'd take part in. He'd started getting his resume together to go back to a day job. Even his button-down shirts had made a reappearance in his closet. The thing was, I'd read all his screenplays and I knew they were great. It was just a matter of time before the world would recognize his talent.

"ISLA had requested my screenplay a while back, and I'd never heard from them," Dad said. "But because I was short-listed for Project Light, an assistant saw my name and title in the trades and actually read it. Then they had Robert read, and he offered me representation a couple of hours ago."

"Dad! That's incredible. I'm just . . ." I started crying. Again. "I'm so proud of you."

He wrapped me in another Dad hug, and Mom got in on it too.

"You made this happen," Dad said, releasing me.

"What? No," I said. "This was all your talent."

He shook his head. "You pushed me to apply to Project Light. You've pushed me through three years of struggle, always believing in me. Soundboarding ideas with me, reading dialogue, all of it."

"If anything, I created the struggle. You would've already been a big name if you'd gone to LA."

"Agree to disagree, Kel," he said. We'd been over this plenty of times before.

"So is this why the two of you seem kinda drunk? Where's the car?" I asked.

"We did have some champagne to celebrate," Mom said. "We took a Lyft back."

These were big splurges for my family, and it was completely uncharacteristic for my mom to day drink, but it was all so well deserved.

"What's the next step?" I asked.

"Well, we're going to wait on the Project Light results," Dad said. "If I don't win, Robert and his assistant are going to send me notes to revise the screenplay to get it in the best shape possible, then he has a couple of producers he wants to pitch it to."

I loved his show-business talk. Absolutely loved that he'd suddenly become an insider like he'd dreamed about.

"Well, I'm always ready to read a revision," I said.

"I'll take you up on that." Dad pinched my chin and I smiled even wider. I'd been smiling so hard, my cheeks hurt. "So tell us about your trip. What did you think of UPenn? How was your night?"

"Oh, would you look at the time," I said, staring at my empty wrist. "Time to be . . . elsewhere."

"Kelsie Marie," Mom said.

I sighed and dragged myself back to the butcher-block island. "It was okay. Eric really loved it though. I wouldn't be surprised if he went there instead of Hopkins."

Mom raised her eyebrows. "That would be a change."

"I know," I said. "He really wants to play football and it is an Ivy, so I hope he gets recruited."

My mom and dad looked at each other and then back at me.

"What?" I said.

I opened the teal cabinets, then the fridge, hoping for something good. If I'd been back on time, I could've gone to lunch with them, but I also wouldn't have patched things up with Bri, so it was well worth staying at UPenn and scrounging through the kitchen now.

"It's just that . . . how do I put this?" Dad said.

"It's a surprise to hear you being nice about Eric," Mom said.

"Love all the support, guys." I did a fake fist pump as I pulled out the ingredients for a mega roast beef sandwich.

"It's just unexpected, that's all," Dad said.

"So you had a good trip?" Mom asked.

I slathered some mayo on the roll. "Yeah. It was . . ."

How could I even sum up the trip between the ridiculous optimism, the near disaster, and the triumph?

"It was good," I said.

"Well, I'm glad. Do you think you'll apply there?" Mom asked.

"Come on." I stopped piling on roast beef. "We don't have the money for me to go there."

"There's financial aid," Mom said.

"And I could sell a screenplay tomorrow," Dad added.

"I know," I said. "But I need to keep my expectations reasonable."

"You're the smartest in your class, Kel," Mom said. "I don't want you to think about money when you apply. We'll figure it out."

It was so nice of them to say, really. And this was the third time they'd said something like that. We'd discussed it twice at our monthly state-of-the-family meetings. They were the best parents in the world, but I was also trying to be a good daughter. They didn't need the financial strain of loans and me hitting them up for pizza money while I was in college.

"We'll see," I said. I finished making my sandwich, cut it in half, and took a big bite.

"Wow," Dad said. "She used your 'we'll see' against you, Dani."

My mom's name was Danielle, but Dad called her Dani.

Mom shot him an unamused glare, then smiled. "We'll see how things go this fall."

She was right. A lot could change in the next few months. A ton had changed since June, and if I'd learned anything from the trip, it was that I needed to stop fighting for things to stay the same.

"I ran into Bri while I was there," I said.

"Oh, really?" Mom's eyebrows hit her hairline. Although I didn't go into detail, she knew we'd had a falling-out. It was impossible to keep it from her since Bri had been a staple in our house and my mom was constantly asking me how she was doing.

"She seemed good," I said. "She was there with her mom."

"Oh," Dad said.

Yeah, my parents weren't wild about Elaine Taylor either. They were super-active PTA-type parents and Elaine was not, but she'd sweep in with her big money and get more praise than my parents, who were always lending a hand.

"So are things . . . okay with you two now?" Mom asked.

I polished off half my sandwich and washed it down with iced tea. Suddenly, my mind flashed to drinking sweet tea with Eric and how he'd accidentally tossed a straw wrapper into my shirt. It had fallen out when I took off my clothes before my shower. I had to try to suppress a smile and a blush from the memory.

"Um, yeah, we're good. Hey, did you know I have a major issue apologizing?" I said.

Mom stared at the ceiling, but it was my dad's nod that got to me. Literally everyone but me knew this.

"Thanks for alerting me to that gem of a characteristic, guys," I said.

"I like that you live your life with certainty," Dad said. "But yes, there have been times where it seemed like apologizing was the absolute last thing you'd do. Death before dishonor and all."

It was my turn to purse my lips and pause before I attacked the second half of my sandwich.

"So did you apologize to Eric?" Mom asked.

"No. Why would I?" I said.

My parents both stared at me. I wiped the corners of my mouth like I had mayo on my face.

"Well, for being so mean to him for all those years when he just liked you," Mom said.

"Excuse me?!" I said.

My dad looked the other way, as if he was now extremely

interested in the living room furniture. Then he wandered into the other room. Coward.

"I mean, he's had a crush on you forever, and you've always been so nasty to him," Mom said. "I wondered if you apologized to him, too."

"You've completely lost touch with reality and should never have champagne," I said.

"Kel." Mom shook her head. "Why do you think he invited you on the trip to UPenn?"

I couldn't really talk to her about our stalker pact, so I attacked her other claim. "He has not had a crush on me since forever."

She sighed like I was her most exhausting child. And unless they'd sold Hanna to a traveling circus that couldn't be true. "He's always looking at you, always choosing you for projects, always asking about you."

"All of that is incorrect," I said.

"All right, Kel. Think what you want." She exhaled and shook her head. Ugh! My mother was telling me I was one hundred percent wrong about everything in life, but she'd let me sit there believing the sky was green if I wanted to.

Moms were The Worst.

"If he asks about me, it's to be polite," I said. "And also because he's a kiss ass who can't help himself."

She shrugged. "It's not really kissing butt to ask how you'd been and if you were going to the party last Saturday."

"What?" I nearly choked on my last bite of sandwich.

"I just don't think it was." Mom poured herself a much-needed glass of water, because what had she even said?

"He asked if I was going to be at the party on Saturday?" I said.

"Yes. He'd been on the fence about going," she said. "I ran into him at the park while I was doing my miles. He was running too."

No one ever told me a thing. Seriously, what use was everyone?

"Why would he ask that?"

"Because he likes you and missed you while he was away." She stared at me, somehow refraining from saying "duh" aloud, but her look said it all.

I stood in stunned silence.

"Darling," my mom said, "I finally won an argument with our daughter!"

"Look at you go, Dani!" Dad said.

I remained in the kitchen alone as my mom joined my dad in the living room. They cuddled on the couch because they were horrible, awful people. But was anything Mom had said true?

Pieces of the night, such as the fact that Eric had really stopped looking for Jessica after he left the flowers, came floating back in my mind. That memory joined with how he'd stood up for me at the frat party, what he'd said at dinner about the day in the park, and, of course, his kiss.

He knew my coffee orders, what I liked to eat, the outfits I wore; he'd been paying attention all this time. The same way I'd been paying attention to him.

But we'd been unable to say anything. Because attraction was hard. Because rejection was worse.

It had been him all this time. And maybe for him it had been me.

The movie *Say Anything* floated through my mind.

Of course.

I took off running up the stairs. I knew exactly what I wanted to do. I just had to find the nerve to do it.

CHAPTER FORTY-FOUR

Hours later and fully sober, my dad drove me over to Carver. He was humming, still in the glow of his success. I, on the other hand, was sweating in the passenger seat, second-guessing everything, down to the ridiculous sign I'd spent two hours making. Eric would see it and laugh at me. I'd be humiliated in front of everyone. I'd have to leave Carver.

Those were pretty much the best-case outcomes.

I slouched in my seat. It wasn't too late to abandon ship. Move out of Saratoga, change my name.

"Why can't I go to the football game?" Hanna pouted from the backseat.

I widened my eyes and stared over at my dad. She was not allowed to come.

"Because the game will go past your bedtime," Dad said.

"But it's Friday and still summer," she whined.

God help me, no eight-year-old demon was going to tag

along on this mission. I'd roll out of the car first.

"And that means it's movie night tonight," Dad said.

Hanna was quiet for a second. "I get to pick," she said.

Dad sighed. Ha! Good luck watching some horrible Disney TV spin-off, guys. The prospect of getting completely shot down by Eric was sounding better by the second.

That was until we pulled up alongside the football field. Then: panic ensued.

The timing was wrong. He'd just broken up with his girlfriend. His world was upside down. Our trip was one thing. Our real lives were another. I was putting him on the spot with my grand gesture. More and more doubts filled my head until I physically grabbed at my skull.

"You okay, Kel?" Dad asked.

"I'm . . . maybe we should just go." The sign was folded up by my feet, leaning against my leg, taunting me.

Dad stared at me. "If you want to turn around and watch *Descendants 3* with us . . . again, you know I'm happy to have you home. But, honey, you're doing a very brave thing, and it's normal to have second thoughts when you put your most valuable asset on the line."

I looked around trying to figure out what he meant. What was my most valuable asset? "My pride?"

"Your heart."

He tucked my hair behind my ear.

Tears welled in my eyes. I refused to cry because I'd put a ton of effort into my makeup. He was right, though. It was my heart on the line, and that was the hardest thing to risk. It had given me cold feet before going up to Bri as well. But Eric had been the one who'd talked me through it, even though I hadn't been nice to him since seventh grade.

"Can we get McDonald's?" Hanna said.

Apparently my melodrama was boring my little sister, but I had to respect her constant hustle.

"We'll see," Dad said. He barely glanced into the back, well aware of the con artist in the backseat. "What's it going to be, Kel?"

I took a deep breath, and before I could talk myself out of it, I opened the car door.

"That's my girl," he said. "Text me when you need a ride back. If you need one."

I gave him some kind of confused smile that was somewhere between "okay" and "what do I even say to that?" then I walked to the field.

I felt a little self-conscious wearing a white dress to a football game, but it was still surprisingly hot out, and I remembered girls getting dressed up for Friday night games. They were usually going out after, but I just wanted to give my proposal the best odds.

One day I'd really have to examine why I thought sundresses shifted the scales in my favor.

I scanned the field and found Eric sitting on the bench. I'd apparently gotten the time of the game wrong. It was already well underway. Our offense had gotten a field goal, and our defense was on the field. Which meant that I was pretty much the only person walking up to the fairly crowded stands.

Awesome. Super incognito.

I went the long way and made eye contact with him. He looked confused for a second, then smiled. My heart felt it, fluttering wildly. Was this how people normally felt when they liked someone? How did they even function?

I shifted my focus to the stairs of the bleachers because I absolutely refused to face-plant in front of everyone.

When I got to the top of the first set of stairs, I was trying to decide on where to sit when I noticed Teagan staring over at me. Her expression was blank before she waved me over. She had the girls she was with slide over to make room.

I passed some kids from school who looked at my dress like I'd grown a second head, then I took the three stairs up to where Teagan was sitting in the center of the stands.

For a second I paused, trying to give her a chance to tell me to go away. That she'd really waved to the ghost behind me.

"Hey, sit," Teagan said.

I plopped down next to her on the warm metal. She was there with two other girls who I sort of knew, in the way that everyone knew each other at Carver, but they were the year below us and on the track team with Teagan.

We watched the defense not do terribly well, but the other team's offense wasn't great either. Eventually, they had to punt back to us.

I sat there paying attention to the game, but also trying to think of what to say to Teagan. There was a lot. But she'd messaged me and she'd waved me over, so she'd already been the bigger person.

"Hey, um, I . . ." Then I trailed off because I was a coward.

I felt her studying me as the cheerleaders ran out to do a little lift maneuver they worked too hard on. Like our football players, our cheerleaders were also from our nerd school, and they were sorely missing Brianna, who used to be front and center.

"I miss Bri," Teagan said.

I blew out a breath. "I do too."

"I know you do." Teagan looked over at me, waiting, like I was an actor who was supposed to say the next line.

We sat in silence again.

"But you don't miss me," she added.

I startled on the bench. "What? Of course I miss you! But it was always just . . . it seemed like we were friends through Bri, and once she was gone, you wouldn't want to be friends with me."

Teagan stared at me. "Have you lost your mind?"

"I mean, the case could be made for that, yeah," I said.

She tilted her head. "We met through Bri, but you really thought we were only friends because of her?"

"I . . . sort of?"

"So, you don't want to be friends with me now that she's gone? I have to lose both of you?"

"What? No. That's not it at all. I thought you weren't talking to me."

She shrugged. "You didn't message. And for a little while I was mad at you for how you'd hurt Bri. But mainly I've just had a lot going on and I thought, if she doesn't want to reach out, whatever."

"I did want to, but I didn't because . . . I'm the worst. What did you have going on?"

"My parents are going to expand the café into the space next door."

"Really? That's awesome! That was totally your idea!" I turned in my seat, fully facing her.

She nodded. "They finally listened to sense, but between getting ready for that, work, and the soccer travel league, I haven't had a ton of free time. And I guess since you didn't reach out even though Bri said you were texting a lot, I figured you didn't want to talk."

I bit my lip, guilt hitting me like a sucker punch to the gut. I really had never tried to be friends with Teagan so much as took her for granted. I grabbed her hand. "I'm really sorry, Tea. It's come to my attention that I'm kind of an asshole."

She let out a long exhale and we watched the game some more.

"So . . . do you still want to be friends with a semi-asshole?" I asked. "One that promises to try a lot harder?"

"That all depends," she said.

"On?" I said. I was willing to do just about anything.

"On you answering my Insta DM." She raised her eyebrows twice, then laughed.

I let out something that was like a snarf-chortle.

"It's . . ." I made some juggling motion with my hands to say: who even knows.

At that moment the center snapped the ball to Eric and he took off running downfield. The entire crowd stood as he passed the defensive line, certain they were in for something special. I took out my camera and recorded him just in time to get him running downfield and dodging two tackles to score a touchdown. The crowd around us went wild. Two clicks later I'd sent the video of his athletics to UPenn recruiting along with his email address (again).

Teagan and I sat back down, and she raised an eyebrow at me.

"Something?" she asked.

"Something," I said.

She did a little motion with her fists. "I knew it! Oh my God, he's had a thing for you since forever, but it always seemed like you hated him. What happened? What changed your mind?"

Why was everyone saying that Eric had liked me for so long? Was this like the apology thing that I just hadn't noticed? And what else wasn't I seeing about myself? About the world? Wasn't I supposed to be so much smarter than this?

"He's had a thing for me forever?" I said.

She shrugged. "Well, yeah."

"He said that?" I said.

"He didn't need to. It's so obvious. He never dates anyone from school, which he says is to keep things simple, but it's always been because he wanted you. You're the Carver enigma."

What in the world? I pointed to my chest. "Me?"

"Yeah, you're, like, scary smart and you have the hottest guy after you and you always just seemed annoyed by it." She paused and laughed. "No one could figure it out."

Eric had said something about not being able to figure me out. I shook my foot so hard that my sandal nearly fell off as adrenaline coursed through me. I was going to do it. After the game I'd show him my sign. I'd take the risk. Maybe Teagan and my parents were right. Only how was I supposed to get through the game? It wasn't even halftime yet.

The defense took the field and did a terrible job. Eric was on the bench looking unsurprised, but every now and then I could swear he was glancing up at me.

Teagan looked from him to me. "Anytime you want to tell me the Eric story though . . ."

I looked over at her with what I'm sure were wild eyes. She scanned my face and then my still shaking foot.

"Maybe over raisin cake at Gladsmith's tomorrow?" she added.

I smiled. "Yeah. And I'll help out with the bakery expansion however I can. You can count on me."

She grinned back, then adjusted her hair and put on her cool façade again.

After the other team scored a touchdown, Eric got ready to retake the field.

"Thanks, by the way," Teagan said.

"For what?" I asked.

"For apologizing. It's cool of you," she said.

"Yeah, apparently I've had a long-standing problem with saying I'm sorry."

She made a face and waved her hand. "Like any genius at Carver ever wants to admit they're wrong? But seriously, I appreciate it."

She hit her shoulder into mine and I bumped her back. It was pretty awesome that she still wanted to be friends, and I'd try my best to deserve it.

It was finally halftime, and the teams got up to go to the opposite sides of the field for their huddles. The coaches and players took their clipboards and folding chairs on the walk to the goalpost. Eric was the last in line. There was no missing that he looked directly up at me and smiled as he went by. And there was no denying the fact that he could now light a fire in my chest from yards and yards away.

CHAPTER FORTY-FIVE

We won. By three points. But still, it was a big victory for Carver to start out with a win. Matt, our ridiculous owl mascot, had taken up break dancing over the summer, so really we could only redeem ourselves with a W.

After the handshakes and the quick local news interviews, it was my moment. Some of the students had cleared out, but an abnormal number of them were still hanging around. And I knew in my bones they'd record me and make me relive this moment for all time.

What the hell was I doing? Texting worked. Texting worked wonders. I could just text him as I left.

"You look off. You okay?" Teagan asked.

"No, I . . . no."

"Do you need a ride?" she asked.

"No, I need to stay and make a fool of myself." I clutched my still-folded-up sign. I was so glad I'd scaled back my original idea of bringing an actual boom box.

"Okay. . . ." She said it slowly.

"I can just text him, right? Texting is cool?"

"I dunno. Depends on what you need to say," Teagan said.

"I need to apologize."

She stared thoughtfully. "Hmm, that's more of an in-person thing, like what you did with me and Bri.

"Well, yes, but I thought you guys wouldn't answer my texts," I said.

"Apologies are better in person, but honestly, you don't have to do it now, in front of everyone. I bet just swinging by his house later will work too. I can give you a ride home, if you want."

"Yeah. Yes. I think that's a much better idea," I said.

I should've sprouted feathers right then and become the new mascot: the Carver Chicken.

"Come on, let's go," she said.

We went down the risers and took the stairs off the bleachers. Unfortunately, I turned back to sneak one last look at Eric. And right at that moment, his gaze connected with mine.

"Hey!" he said.

He jogged after us. I couldn't exactly run away from him again, so instead I stayed put. Teagan froze a few feet in front of me.

"Hey," I said.

"I didn't expect to see you," Eric said. "Hey, Teagan."

"Great game, Eric." She twirled her hair, obviously unable to stop herself.

Then we were all silent. Teagan looked at him, then at me, then back at him, then took three comically large steps away from us.

Super smooth.

"Yeah, I . . ." I stared down at the pavement. This was such a bad frigging idea. "I made you something," I muttered.

Note: it wasn't really the bravery tour de force I'd expected, but at least I'd said it.

"You did? What is it?" he asked.

I made an *eep* sound and bit my lip.

"Is it that?" He pointed to the sign that was still folded in half.
"It . . . well . . ."

"Or does it have something to do with an email I got earlier from UPenn?" he asked with a smile.

That gave me the courage to make eye contact with him.

"You got an email from UPenn?" I said.

He nodded. "They'd seen me at camp, but someone sent my info and the *Saratogian* article to their recruitment office."

"Well, that person sounds delightful and very sexy," I said. "And she probably just sent them footage of you running in the touchdown."

He smiled slowly. "I like her. What's going on with the sign?"

Ugh.

I took a deep breath and opened the sign, then lifted it above my head. Eric stared at it, taking in the boom box I'd painted and the words: "I'm sorry. It's always been you."

My homage to *Say Anything*. To what we'd talked about—if he even remembered our drunken conversation. And as I stood there in a dress, holding up a sign that a bunch of people could see, I could not have felt more ridiculous. But you do strange and embarrassing things for the people you love.

Eric stood there with his eyes wide.

"I've been . . . I've been trying to find a way to say this," I said. "How I hadn't even realized . . . This isn't good timing. I know it, I just . . ." I stared at the ground and lowered the sign. "Never mind."

The pavement at our field was fantastically interesting really.

"Kelsie," he said.

After an eon, I looked up at him.

"I love it," he said.

"You do?" I asked. "Well, I think this went great. Smoother than expected."

He laughed. "Sometimes things are better unplanned."

Eric reached forward and took the sign from me.

"I'd like to take you to a movie tomorrow," he said, wrapping his other arm around my waist. "And compete against you every day. And have you push me to be the best I possibly can be. Always. And support you when you need it and fall asleep talking to you every night because I need it."

I stared at him, my resolve to not ruin my makeup was crumbling.

"How was your speech better than mine? I planned this moment out for hours," I said.

"Because I've been thinking about it since I heard you say that you were into me in the car."

I pushed my palm into his chest. "Creeper! You were awake!"

"I was," he shrugged. "I'm glad I was."

And really, what could I say to that?

I let my hands drift up his chest to wrap my arms around his neck. He looked down at me with the dreamiest stare I could imagine. And even though I couldn't see my own face, I knew I was looking at him in the same way.

"Am I . . . still Edison?" I asked.

"Oh, you definitely are, but I'd still like to kiss you—for the second time."

I didn't have the slightest bit of doubt as I perched on my tiptoes and met his lips with mine.

Kelsie's Log of Success

ONE DAY AFTER

I have a friend. I have a best friend. And I have a boyfriend. And I have a totally uncertain future. And I'm okay with that. Great, actually.

ACKNOWLEDGMENTS

Thank you to everyone at Simon & Schuster Books for Young Readers, for your support, hard work, and amazing talents, especially my editor extraordinaire, Krista Vitola, whose skill and insights helped mold this story into one I'm so proud of. Special thanks to Krista Vossen and Sandra Chiu for capturing Eric and Kelsie so perfectly.

Thank you to Lauren Abramo and Jennifer Ung for believing in me and helping me become a better writer. Thank you to Stephanie Kim and New Leaf for taking this journey with me. And thank you to Tova at Salt & Sage for your guidance on crafting Eric's character.

Thank you, John, for talking through the hard things with me, for the shoulder rubs and walks, and for being my rock and giving my heart a home.

Thank you to my fantastic writer friends, especially Karen McManus, who continues to inspire and amaze me. Thank you to Jenn Dugan for all your advice and love in my post-debut spiral. Thank you to Germany Jen for your insight and counterbalance, and for never failing to champion my career. Thank you to Justin Reynolds, June Tan, Caroline Richmond,

Misa Sugiura, Sabina Kahn, Sarah Suk, and Fallon DeMornay for your friendship and WhatsApp secret sharing. Thank you to Dahlia Adler, Phil Stamper, Anne Ursu, and CW for all your support for my debut and beyond!

Thank you so much to all the educators, librarians, book bloggers, BookTokers, Bookstagrammers, and all reviewers who spent time in my worlds.

Thank you to my babies, my sunshine and heart. Your pride in me does more than words can express. Thank you for always understanding when I need to write and for only mildly scheming iPad time out of it. Thank you to my mom for allowing me to live through my unapologetic teenage years and for truly being a great friend now. Thank you to Matt, Jessica, Susan, and Molly for your friendship, support, and shoulders to cry on. Thank you to my sister, who isn't a gremlin, and to Gregg for wrangling ours.

Last but not least, thank you, my readers, for taking this journey with me. I wish I could tell Laura thank you for all those years together. I hope you tell your best friend today.